Finding Victoria

Moments that Matter

Adelaide Rix

100% of the proceeds from this book
will be equally donated to

Parkinson's UK
Registered charity England and Wales no. 258197
and in Scotland no.SC037554
https://www.parkinsons.org.uk/

In aid of

&

People's Trust for Endangered Species UK
Registered charity no. 274206
https://ptes.org/

people's
trust for
endangered
species

*The opinions expressed in this book are not necessarily those
of Parkinson's UK or of People's Trust for Endangered Species.

All rights reserved. Printed in the United States of America. No part of this book may be used or reproduced in any manner whatsoever without the written permission of the author. This work is fiction, and any references or similarities to actual people and events are coincidental or very loosely based on people and places known by the author.
Finding Victoria Copyright © 2025 by Adelaide Rix
Photography and cover design by Adelaide Rix

ISBN: 979-8-21870-811-5
ISBN (ebook): 979-8-21870-812-2

DEDICATION

For Robert E. Cazenove,
Who charmed me near the buses
on a London street corner in August 1990
and changed my life, not once but twice.
Our decades of shared and loving
Victoria moments
continue to fill my heart.
My Bobby, My Merlin…
It was always you.
Sometimes life gives us second chances,
perhaps even three, when it's meant to be.
Never doubt -- I was always and still am ALL IN.
Absence DOES make the heart grow fonder,
But so does being together.
Happy 35th. Happy 63rd.
With love, friendship, gratitude, and more.

&

For Bunny
With love and respect, RIP

DEFINITION

Finding Victoria: When you appreciate the beautiful value in and understand the meaningful impact of a chance meeting, a trivial decision, a brief moment, or a subtle sign from the universe.

TABLE OF CONTENTS

	Acknowledgements	i
	Preface	iii
1	Finding Victoria	1
2	Angus McGregor	15
3	The Digby 5	21
4	How Gordon Ramsay Saved My Marriage	32
5	Bunny Magic	47
6	In the Land of Beatrix	57
7	Tit for Tat	71
8	Lords, Lads, and Lairds	85
9	Life of the Party	97
10	The Margaret Matrix	105
11	The Girls' Club	113
12	The Fox Whisperer	123
13	Erasing Mr. Corrigan	137
14	Last Train Out of Bognor Regis	147
15	"And the Award Goes To…"	159
16	"I Think That I Shall Never See"	166
17	Come to Jesus Moment	175
18	Fish & Chips and Warrior Therapy	185
	Epilogue	197

Finding Victoria

ACKNOWLEDGEMENTS

I would like to thank Larry Meachum for our many Sunday morning conversations about writing and life, over omelets and coffee in Depot Town; those conversations in Michigan have lingered for over four decades.

Many thanks to elementary school friend William Routt for a much-needed and unexpected persuasive literary nudge while conversing at the bar (as adults, of course). Thanks for your service!

Finding Victoria

Finding Victoria

PREFACE

Writing is like anything we put off for another day; the roadblock is often laziness, but mostly it is FEAR. We fear failure, criticism, or disapproval. We fear offending someone. We fear our vulnerabilities. We fear that the intention or the message will be misconstrued. We wonder if we have the discipline to follow through on such a deeply felt personal endeavor. Retreating is easy.

Many years ago, a friend told me people should only write if they have something to say. It is one of the most intimidating pieces of advice I have ever been given, but so basic. It was promptly followed on my end by a lifelong pause on writing, filled with many years of procrastination and fear, much in poet T.S. Eliot's J. Alfred Prufrock fashion: "Do I dare? and, Do I dare?" After all, what exactly did I have to say?

But recently I started to think about how technology, social media, and now, the dawn of AI (artificial intelligence) have openly invited just about anyone into the arena of published self-expression, and although novice writers have found great success with publication and sales, many do not really have much to say, and one has to ask is it even them who is writing and saying it or is it some chatbot?

Finding Victoria

I now view the art of writing as premised with more focus on this question: How does one write with authenticity? Viewing it from that perspective still makes dipping my toe in as a writer intimidating, but I believe if I can tap into the bucket of my emotional well, then I will have something to say, and it will be truly authentic.

If you are looking for a unique story, you will not find it in these pages. Mankind has been telling the same stories throughout the ages; they are just packaged differently. Look at cave paintings or other later images from antiquity: There is connection or empathy with nature, expression of anger in warring elements, or fear in persecution scenes…even romance. Stories are told of the human condition and emotions. Those do not change over time. The main catalyst for a story? Love and grief, chiefly. **Love inspires; grief motivates.** What could be more universal, more real? Those feelings run deep, and they can't be faked. Authentic. All good stories contain both on different levels. They work in tandem.

Finding Victoria attempts to capture minor but significant points in life's narrative that remind us that there are beautiful and joyful emotions and experiences, even in ordinary moments and that we should recognize and appreciate how the randomness and serendipity of life can often especially illuminate the light of hope or provide a feeling of peace, even on a small scale…silver linings, in some cases.

Moments matter – all of them. A single incident, a few words, or a chance meeting can direct our sails forever or turn the tide on a sea of troubles. Fragments of a joyous memory can support and impact us decades later when we most need them, in the clutches of heartache or loneliness. Perhaps you notice a very personal song comes on the radio at the precise moment you need it for comfort or to bring a smile? Or the name of someone you've been thinking about continues to appear throughout the day? The potential for hope, joy, and reassurance

Finding Victoria

is always there. And who couldn't use some of that?

I have wandered the halls of the Tate National Gallery in London countless times and viewed the same paintings over and over, seeing something new each time: the positioning of the hands of Ophelia looming above me or the pleading eyes of the female lover in *A Huguenot,* both by artist John Everett Millais. I am overcome with each encounter as if viewing the works for the first time. The art moves me; it sparks me. That freshness, that newness of emotion…it's what we crave as humans. Feeling alive. I leave the gallery with optimism every time. The Tate is my required first stop each time I go to London, like filling up my tank for the travels ahead. It means admiring emotion in any form of expression and truly SEEING and FEELING it. Connecting to it.

The good news is that there are sources for that feeling all around us every day; we just need to immerse ourselves in them. I call that process, and those feelings, *Finding Victoria,* because I get that charge when I am in or near Victoria Station in London, not unlike my visits to the Tate, for reasons you will soon discover.

These moments are dopamine hits we take for granted; they can come from many inconspicuous and often mundane, and ordinary places. Perhaps it is in coordinating the weekly shop with a partner, scouring the aisles together for items to check off a list, and then getting home and meticulously shelving the groceries, each item in its proper place, right down to folding the bags methodically and intentionally storing them for the next time. Satisfaction in a team effort. Or lovers hanging clothes together on the line with a prescribed orderly system. The clipping of the clothespins on the line after shaking the damp clothes out briskly in the summer air. And listening to the morning mail drop coming through the front door mail slot, while the dog scrambles to make a play at it with ferocious but harmless barking. Daily events and routine things that occur

Finding Victoria

worldwide; nothing extraordinary about them, right? Can those things be so significant?

In contrast, imagine those same routines but now you are alone (no partner, no lover, no affectionate dog), you suddenly understand their significance. You miss the impish smile of your partner as he playfully persuades you to add olives with cheese cubes or tiramisu to the shopping cart as forbidden treats not on the list; you long for the fresh scent of the laundry waving in the wind on the line as you hope to receive a loving wink from a partner who peers at you from the row of socks hanging on the line, and you hate the silence of the postal delivery hitting the front hall floor from the mail slot when the guard dog is no more. The memories of those seemingly uneventful moments can and do linger for a lifetime; you want to recreate them for the feelings they inspire and the smiles they bring in retrospect. Those powerful vehicles and purveyors of joy. You are empty without them. Lonely.

We savor these "Victoria moments"…the daily 'victories,' to play on the word a bit. They carry meaning…sometimes, so powerful that they change the trajectory of our lives. And they don't let go. A chance meeting because we decided to stop at the library instead of going straight home…simple words, gestures, actions. *Moments.*

Subscribe to Ferris Buehler's admonishment to "stop and look around once in a while" approach to life. We are all disciples of that on some level. Exercising mindfulness and compassion for others prompts meaningful enlightenment in this busy beehive of life. This book speaks to those things we should take more notice of and find purpose in…revel in their rich goodness, find joy and peace in the arbitrary things, and feel gratitude for them. Stopping to smell the roses; finding your zen; being present in the moment; whatever you call it, it all matters because otherwise, as Buehler notes, we might miss something. And that would be tragic.

Finding Victoria

Regardless of what your beliefs are grounded in, you may ask of coincidental moments, "Is there some master plan here at work?" Is the universe speaking to us in subtle ways? God? A higher power? Perhaps. Or is it all grounded in objective scientific laws of statistics? That is for you to ultimately decide, but if I have prompted you to pause even briefly to "look around" and take it all in, consider it, savor it, then I have achieved my purpose. It is up to you to find meaning and connection.

One challenge in this exercise is worth mentioning: The memory is a tricky databank. Its veracity is threatened daily by distractions, disease, the aging process, and other influences. How do we capture and retain a singular moment so absolutely? Despite our best efforts to bottle the essence of a pure memory or moment, it's like trying to catch smoke unless we capture it on our phones or write it down in a diary. However, take heart. Maybe we don't recall the exact color of the shirt a man was wearing, or the name of the perfume that danced in her hair. But we do remember how someone's heartfelt laughter made us feel as they watched a comedy show on television, or savoring the scent that still transports you to a quiet chateau on a lake when she unexpectedly asked you to marry her, and you sincerely said, "Yes" without hesitation ...the heart remembers.

Thematically, this book takes a look at moments through a British-American lens, but it could be through ANY lens. So, read these stories with emotions in mind. Connect to them. Let them take you to a place in your heart that says, "Ah, yes! I know or can imagine what that feels like!" "Wow, that comment or action had a real impact on my life..." or "I know someone like that." Moments, people, places that mean something.

Thus, back to T.S. Eliot..."So let us go then, you and I" to find our Victoria moments. But I suggest you don't actively seek them out; relax and let them happen...they will find you. Be still. Just be observant and aware when they present

Finding Victoria

themselves to you, and embrace them when they unfold whether you are standing on the threshold of Victoria Station or elsewhere.

And whatever you do…don't let go.

Adelaide Rix
Written in celebration of a special anniversary & birthday
August 2025

Finding Victoria

1 Finding Victoria

    The distinct acrid smell of bus exhaust filled the air of a warm August day filled with gaggles of tourists scurrying through the London streets, the deep-droning hum of their roller suitcases scraping and rumbling the pavement near Victoria Station, barely a fifteen-minute walk from Buckingham Palace. The long overnight flight from the States and then the subsequent bus ride from Heathrow were motivation for her to stretch her legs and do some walking. It was a confusing world to Bernie. She felt like a twenty-five-year-old Connecticut Yankee in King Arthur's court.

    With a large, quilted red floral bag on her shoulder and a backpack carried by its worn, frayed handle, she surveilled the streets searching for some kind of perpendicular sense to the layout of the roads before her. Only steps away from the station, she knew her destination (a bed and breakfast) was only two blocks away, except these weren't technically "blocks" really. Unfolding the map, she studied it like she was examining bacteria under a microscope. This was 1990, and Google maps was still decades away from public consumption. She re-adjusted the Vera Bradley bag on her shoulder, tucked the map into a pocket, and started walking, figuring she could read the street signs and easily sort out where to go.

    Hmmmm...street signs, or more appropriately, "Where the

Finding Victoria

hell WERE they?" This would not be easy.

Bernie, short for Bernadette, had been planning this trip for a year, carefully calculating and budgeting, from her nanny job, every British pound necessary to spend for two weeks in the city. She eagle-eyed the exchange rate every day. Her first trip out of North America.

She had memorized the Frommer's and Fodor guides from cover to cover. A travel virgin. For a young person, it was an exciting time; independence and the unknown lay ahead of her. Newly engaged and transitioning from nanny to a formal career in education, she concluded this trip could be her last hurrah to be on her own, at least for a while. And part of her just felt as if she needed some breathing room before plunging into marriage and a career change…a mental catharsis for a few weeks.

Even the bus ride into the city from Heathrow Airport to Victoria was thrilling to her. An exotic, dark-haired man in colorful robe-like clothing, sitting opposite her on the bus, must have recognized her starstruck expression as she peered out the window, a small grin curling in the corner of her lips.

"First time in London?" he broached in a friendly tone and unfamiliar accent. He had only a briefcase at his feet and a rolled newspaper in his hand.

She smiled broadly. "Yes!"

"Are you on holiday?" he again correctly surmised. He leaned in.

She paused over the use of the word "holiday," and confirmed, "I'm on vacation."

"You're American," he mused and smirked, to which she nodded.

Her introverted nature was shelved for the time being, and she wanted to talk more to this stranger. It was an opportunity to test the waters of being completely anonymous yet actively social. The bus was full; no one else was making eye contact. Chatting with strangers was not in her nature, but she could be anyone she wanted to be here. She barely spoke with anyone since leaving home, and she longed for conversation.

"I'm Michael," he offered his hand across to her. She decided he had warm eyes and responded in kind with her own hand.

"Bernie." She surprised herself that she gave up her nickname so easily, which was reserved for only very close friends and family. Most people used her full name, Bernadette.

The new acquaintance held her hand a few seconds more than what was politely comfortable, making direct eye contact that held for a moment longer as well. He must have sensed some reticence on her part and took the lead in continuing the chat to put her at ease.

"Have you ever met Madonna?"

"Madonna?" She couldn't tell if he was being serious or just trying to break the ice. Laughing in response, "Oh, no."

"How long are you here in the UK?"

"Oh, about two weeks."

Then he paused, looking more closely at her as if trying to read her mind. "You are a nurse? A teacher?"

There was nothing of obvious note that would indicate she belonged to either of those professions. She was dressed in simple jean shorts, a plain short-sleeved pink shirt, and sneakers. Michael's earnest inquiries drew her in even more with what he had to say. There was no evidence of age in his jet-black hair or smooth chocolate complexion, but his hands gave away some years. She guessed him to be in his forties.

"Well, almost a teacher. I'm actually a nanny right now," she was impressed with the accuracy of his guess after such a brief introduction. That is eerily close, she thought.

"You have a compassionate aura," he smiled, his gaze following an imaginary outline of her.

There was a polite silence that typically would have remained, but then Bernie picked up the mantle of conversation.

"Are you from London?"

"Just here for business," Michael said, shaking his head. "I am from Iran originally, but I live in France now. I'm here often,

Finding Victoria

though. I usually taxi into the city, but today I felt like enjoying a bus ride."

"Oh, how long does it take to get into the city?" Bernie asked.

"About thirty to forty minutes, depending on traffic…and tourists," he added with a wink.

The door was opened for the conversation to carry on for the rest of the bus journey. They touched on the politics of the time: Iraq and Saddam Hussein, and of celebrity royalty, Princess Diana. Michael voiced very personal concerns over the events occurring in the Middle East. Iraq was threatening Kuwait, relations between Iran and Iraq were tenuous, and the United States was making its presence known in the Gulf. It was a topic and region that seemed so very far removed from her. Bernie felt ignorant about the details of the events of which he spoke, but she felt the raw and passionate emotions in his expressions. Then, it was toward the end of the ride when he said something rather random, but unforgettable, similar to the left-field Madonna question earlier.

"You must watch the movie *Rochester Row*. You will enjoy it."

"Okay," she replied, waiting for more, interested in details.

But the bus was stopping, and the passengers were hustling to grab their belongings to disembark. Again, he extended his hand as he stood up.

"It was a pleasure meeting you, Bernie. Enjoy London. And watch that movie! Don't forget. *Rochester Row*," with an added emphasis on the latter suggestion, with the smile of the Cheshire Cat, as he vanished among the throng of travelers.

She quickly scrawled his name and the title of the movie down on a small notebook she carried, then gathered her bags to join the herd. She wanted to chronicle her journey, thus the handy notebook. Stepping away from the bus, she looked around, trying desperately to avoid being identified as the neophyte American traveler. No camera hanging around her neck, no New York Yankees hat, no t-shirt with a university

Finding Victoria

name splashed across her chest. She was ready.

Now...Where were the damn street signs? Finally, after several minutes of reluctantly pulling out her street map and scouring the street names, she spotted the inconspicuous labels on the sides of the corner buildings. She chose a street she knew was close to her lodging, Eccleston, and started walking, making a casual turn. People scurried past her. Another block. The bags were getting heavier. One more street; they all seemed to have names that began with "E". There was Eccleston Place and Eccleston Street. Not the same. Elizabeth Street and Elizabeth Bridge. She wiped her brow in the August sun. How many blocks had she walked? Twenty to thirty minutes passed. Her pride in check, she refused to take out the map.

She scanned the crowds looking for a potential friendly face who might be able to give her directions. Ironically, a small older woman in a burgundy and gold sari tapped her on the shoulder and asked for help finding the Victoria bus station, only to be met with a shrug and "I'm sorry" from Bernie. More walking. At last, Ebury! But the victory was short-lived when she discovered Ebury Mews was not Ebury Street. Eventually, she found her way. Victorian row houses, each a little different in color and décor, were laid out before her. Exhausted from the flight, the bus, and the marathon walk, she checked in with the priority of getting something to eat and taking a nap. It was only eleven in the morning, and there was a whole city to devour.

However, the best-laid plans often go awry, and she settled on a wine bistro on the corner for lunch, where she engaged in involuntary head-bobs practically into her salad, trying to stay awake; she was a jet lag rookie. The young waitress, with an Eastern European accent softly tapped her on the shoulder in the middle of Bernie's pronounced head-drop.

"Can I get you anything else, Miss?"

Startled, Bernie jerked up in her posture. "No, no...thank you. But I'll take the check, please." For a half-second, she had forgotten where she was. She had no idea what the rules were

Finding Victoria

for tipping, but better safe than sorry, so she left a ten-pound note. Probably too much, but she would sort out the etiquette later.

She settled in her bed for a short rest, but it turned into a seventeen-hour power nap that ushered in the next morning. However, Bernie felt rejuvenated and ready for her first day in London. She was not sure what a full English breakfast meant, but she made her way down to the guest dining area to find a feast of sausages, eggs, baked beans, potatoes, mushrooms, tomatoes, and an array of jams. It was amusing that the toast had its own metal-framed holder. The English are so "proper," she concluded. It gave breakfast credibility.

"I could definitely get used to this!" she shared with another guest, who was getting coffee beside her and did not seem awake, as she heaped her plate with mushrooms.

The walk toward Victoria Station was an easier trek, now that Bernie better understood the illogical layout of the city roads, and she realized it should only have been about a five to ten-minute walk the previous day. Victoria would be her home base for any ventures hereafter. It was her safe place, her comfort zone. A place she could always come back to as a recognizable starting place. It seemed to be the center of the ripple of life in this part of London. Finding Victoria would be the default if all else failed.

The famous red double-decker buses lined up at nearby Grosvenor Gardens, and like any visitor, she felt a tour bus ride was the best place to start to get the lay of the land. Despite a few raindrops, she sat on the open top level of the red tour bus, listening attentively to the guide, Arlo, who was articulating on landmarks and events: the history of the Great Fire that started on Pudding Lane, the soapbox speeches of those who held court in Hyde Park, the Changing of the Guard at Buckingham Palace. She remained on the bus tour for its entirety.

"How many here are from the UK?" Arlo inquired on his microphone, counting a few unenthusiastic hands that went up.

Finding Victoria

"How about Americans?"

Bernie put up the lone hand. Mistake.

"Ahhhh, we have a Yank in our midst!" Arlo rejoiced. He could use some political punchlines he had been practicing in recent trips that humorously targeted Americans. They fell flat.

When the tour ended, Bernie politely thanked her host and tipped him generously. She decided it was time to explore on her own. But mostly she was people-watching, paying close attention to the street signs and their relationship to Victoria, so she could later find her way back. Victoria Station would be her North Star, the center of her London compass for navigation. Relying on only a vague sense of direction, Bernie headed northeast. She recited the street names to herself as an oral exercise: Hudson's Place, Wilton Road, Victoria Street…

The sound of so many languages and accents around her intrigued her, unlike home, and so much was new. The heavy and deep bonging of Big Ben washed over her in Westminster. She stared up at the tower, or rather the Clock Tower, as she learned from Arlo. She had no idea that Big Ben was actually the bell. Brits probably knew that, she thought. The whole area near Parliament vibrated with life and activity, and protestors. "There is No Planet B" and "Extinction is Forever!" signs roused the crowds. She marveled at the architecture of the buildings of political power and walked in the footsteps of her ancestors; one had even worked in the House of Lords.

The day had been a stimulus overload. It was a "good" tiredness that was beginning to tug at her. Time to head back to Ebury to regroup and find a place for dinner. It had been a successful first day and exhilarating in a way. Bernie's life responsibilities faded into the background, and she was focusing on just being in the moment. As she approached Victoria, there loomed a fresh horde of tourists emerging from the station. It was then that a vigorous pull on her arm, with an invitation and pitch to take a bus tour, stopped her in her tracks. A moment.

In that split second, the Robert Frost poem "The Road

Finding Victoria

Not Taken" was conjured. Typically, she would have said, "No thanks," to the tugger, and would have continued on her way. After all, she had just taken the same tour that morning. But this smiling young man, who would be her tour guide and looked to be about her age, with his sweeping blond hair and a mischievous smile, was determined not to take no for an answer. The very late afternoon made for anemic numbers of tourists and passengers for tours, and he was likely trying to make his daily quota.

"But I just took this tour this morning," Bernie politely countered; nonetheless, she unexpectedly paused and was open to listening to his next spiel.

"But you didn't take MY tour," he teased. "You can get off at any stop if you aren't enjoying it. No charge. I will tell you things you have never heard before. I promise you will get your money's worth."

She decided to take the road less traveled by and got on the bus. What the hell? She was heading back to the B&B anyhow. How could she have known that precise moment would set the stage for so many events in her life? *A moment.*

There were only a few people on the bus, but the driver, Gerald, and the guide who tugged her arm, whose name was Simon, got started with their supposed show-stopping performance. Bernie sat once again on the open top, only this time the rain had stopped, and the sun was out. Simon stood only a few feet from her, tested her microphone by blowing on it, and smiled generously at her. Was he flirting? she thought. Well, yes, that's part of the salesmanship; she answered her own question. She would enjoy it all the same. There was something so thoughtful yet playfully silly about him; she liked that.

Then the show began with a subtle wink toward Bernie. It was quite a different presentation from Arlo's. Passing by St. Clements Church, Simon broke out in tune with "Oranges and lemons, sing the bells of St. Clements…" and he told some anecdote about the origin of the song, which seemed a stretch

Finding Victoria

and not what Arlo had mentioned earlier. The Pudding Lane story was embellished, some inappropriate but hilarious stories were shared about Henry VIII, and a few colorful and satirical comments were made about other countries and their relationship with England, with most targeting the United States.

Bernie felt like she was getting a private tour despite the laughter and engagement from the few other passengers in the background. Simon's spotlight seemed to be on her, and for once, she reveled in the attention. He was very animated and full of life. Part of the show. She would give him a decent tip because she was indeed getting her money's worth as promised. He was tall and had a handsome face. There was something very sexy about the line of his nose. The bus eventually slowed, approaching Victoria Station once again.

"And if you have enjoyed this tour, please let your driver, Gerald, know by tipping well," Simon wrapped up to the passengers, as the bus returned to the starting place at Victoria Station. "And of course, if you feel I've taught you something new and interesting, tip me as well. I appreciate your attention. Have a good evening!"

Bernie had many coins in her purse and clanked them into the palm of Simon's hand once outside the bus. He shook his head as if offended and gave them back to her. "No, no charge for you," he smiled. "What are you doing later?" he asked.

Again, she contradicted her modus operandi and automatically said, "Nothing," rather than "I am busy."

"Fabulous!" he grabbed the brochure in her hand, produced a pen, and wrote something on it: "Constitution 7p.m." "Meet me there. It's not far from here." He drew a precise little map with directions, verbally reiterated the streets to get there, and gave her no time to change her mind. He gently kissed her on the lips and went back to the buses.

"What just happened?" thought Bernie. British hospitality? Again, her attitude was "Why not?" and she rushed off to Ebury Street to reconstitute herself.

Finding Victoria

Bernie was nervous as she changed her clothes. This meeting with a stranger was so unlike her. Instead of the long plait, Bernie opted to let her hair down, literally and figuratively. A little touch-up on the make-up was also in order, and perhaps a change of shoes? Checking her watch, she left a little early, in case she got lost, which was a strong possibility. After some meandering from Victoria Station, she tracked the streets to finally lead her to the pub. Seven o'clock with drinks at The Constitution. Simon was already there, seated on a picnic bench outside the entrance in the same white t-shirt and rumpled navy-blue shorts he had on earlier. He must have come directly from work, she realized. And she noticed again the straight line of his nose that was quite attractive as he perused the drinks menu.

She was greeted with a very wide grin when she approached the table. "Your directions were perfect," she said to Simon, who immediately stood respectfully at her arrival.

"Very nice to see you again," his eyes swallowed her.

"Just get off work?" she asked.

"Gerald just dropped me off. What can I get you to drink?"

"Surprise me. I'll have what you're having."

"You like ale? Lager?" he seemed intrigued that she opened herself to experimentation and discovery.

Bernie shrugged, "Whatever…" They both laughed, and he ordered.

The conversation was smooth. No awkward silences. The pair seemed as if they were two old friends who instinctively guided each other on topics, one to another, and then on to the next.

One beer turned into two, which turned into dinner at a nearby restaurant called Grumbles. The conversation was incessant and not lacking in laughter. More drinks were brought to the table. There was a joke about haggis that Bernie did not fully get, but as soon as he explained it was sheep's intestines, they both erupted in interminable laughter, magnified by the alcohol, but sincere just the same. Simon spread some coins out

Finding Victoria

on the table at dinner to explain British currency and the denominations. He was holding court and enjoying the attention of his naïve but captive American companion.

Bernie did not want the evening to end. They strolled the streets afterward for a late night watching old '70s movies at Simon's apartment with his roommates on Churton Street. There was something so comfortable, so natural with this stranger. The world was different now. Maybe it was the beer? Something of magnitude was clearly happening, and it felt right to Bernie. Pure. She had never felt more relaxed, more herself with anyone. No expectations. No inhibitions.

After that evening, Bernie's well-planned itinerary basically went out the window. When Simon was not working, he was sharing his city with Bernie. Her trip was flipped on its head. The fortnight was filled with exuberance and laughter among the cultural intersections. Simon continued to teach her the nuances between the UK and the States. And she staunchly defended her patriotism for her own politics and country, but always with humor. She awkwardly became acclimated to keeping the fork in her left hand at meals as he demonstrated. He held her hand firmly as a safety measure while they walked through the city, cautioning her to turn and look first to the right for traffic while crossing roads. And he laughed when she was quite ignorant of what it meant to order still or sparkling water.

It was an education for Bernie. She felt very inept and vulnerable. He again ensured her safety by walking on the side closest to the traffic as a barrier to any mishap. She took his arm. Her attraction to the city and Simon was intense, consolidated in a kaleidoscope of colorful and sensational emotions. He was so many things she was not: extroverted, self-assured, a magnet for attention with many friends. And there was romance. Was it a fleeting affair? Perhaps. Surely, he had executed this sort of flirtation and seduction script before? She didn't care. They gave real joy to each other, contentment. She held him tightly on the back of his motorcycle through the streets of Chelsea. He

Finding Victoria

grasped her hand tightly across restaurant tables. They shared bicycle rides through Battersea Park, stopping occasionally to walk alongside each other in conversations about life and the world.

One night, they wandered down a side street not far from Victoria, where an Italian restaurant was tucked away safely from tourists. As he held her hand at the table, he commented, "Our hands are the same."

She, too, noticed the similarities in the length of their fingers, the shape of their nails. "Hmmm, what do you suppose that means?" she asked playfully.

"That we must be related! Ahhhh, I may have just slept with my cousin!" followed by more of their unisoned laughter. She withdrew her hand sharply in feigned disgust, but then returned it to his. More laughter.

"It means, perhaps, that maybe we were meant to be together," she suggested and waited for a response.

"Ahhh, yes, you are the great romantic, aren't you?" He smiled but said nothing more.

On the day before her departure for home, she later recalled him speaking of their new connection. He seemed confident they were to be linked somehow, moving forward.

They were sitting outside of a café, and he intensely made eye contact with her over the table after a prolonged silence when he said to her with sincerity, "You will be like that comfortable jersey one cannot part with. It's all new in your twenties, and you enjoy it. By your thirties, it's showing some wear, but still a mainstay item in your wardrobe and vibrant. By your forties, it becomes second nature to grab it from your wardrobe; it's reliable. In your fifties, people expect to see you wearing it; it is part of your identity. In your sixties and seventies?" he paused here, and then, "The idea of being without it is heartbreaking."

It seemed almost prophetic to her. Comforting. Wisdom from a life well-lived, even though Simon was not yet thirty. This may have been code for he was aware of and acknowledging their connection. Bernie was comforted by that. He was not always verbally direct when it came to his feelings.

"So, we are to be like tired old sweaters to each other after we have lived our lives?" she teased. He nodded affectionately.

Later, when she thought of his remarks, she sighed at the last comment… "being without" him. She felt empty already, and it was starting to sink in that she was leaving London…and Simon.

Simon stirred something in her. Bernie thought about what was awaiting her at home. The physical distance had given her clarity. Wedding plans; her footing most of the bills; his neglect; her working two jobs. What had she been thinking? How could so much have changed in just a short period of time?

The final morning in London, she and Simon walked to Victoria together: he, for work on the buses, and she, to leave the UK. The tears welled up without warning for her. Before boarding her bus to Heathrow, with chains of melancholy in tow, she wiped a tear from her cheek as he confidently looked her in the eyes and stated, "You will return." And in the manner and tone he said it, she believed him.

Bernie boarded her bus and sat by the window, watching who seemed to be her complementary other half on the street below, and blew him a kiss. She cried quietly most of the flight home, but it was when she opened the gift he gave her that the other passengers became aware of her stifled sobbing. It was a silly tankard with their names crudely etched on it, with the date. A last-minute but sentimental memento. "Why did this hurt so much?" she thought. After only two weeks. Was that even possible? What was happening?

The domino effect on her life had started. The trip gave her the courage to break off the engagement to her fiancé when she returned home to the States. It was the necessary decision for what might have been a disastrous union. And true to Simon's remark, Bernie did return to London, many times over the years and decades, with Victoria Station always at the center.

But the truly surprising aftershock came when, several years

Finding Victoria

after her first arrival in 1990, she finally watched the movie *Rochester Row*. Blockbuster had it, and late one night and alone, she absorbed it. It was about a young single woman who goes off to Europe on a vacation and meets a foreign man in France. They become infatuated with each other, and all her plans become a spontaneous series of beautiful moments spent getting to know the man and his friends. She ultimately decides to stay in the country. Bernie could not believe it. Michael somehow knew. It was HER story.

As the credits scrolled the screen, Bernie recognized a name among the actors. The best friend of the protagonist was played by actor Christopher Glynne. Later, she would learn that he and her Simon were cousins! What are the chances? Coincidence? Bernie's mind floated back to the bus ride with Michael on that first day in London.

And then some years later, when she watched the movie a second time, her fair-haired husband Simon slept peacefully beside her as she stroked his hair. She was very much aware and reminded of her Victoria moments every day…moments that might have passed her by had she kept walking past the tour buses on a hot August day.

Finding Victoria

2 Angus McGregor

    The sweet spot of grocery shopping times? Sunday at 7 a.m. The Sainsbury parking lot on Wilton Road in the city of London is dotted with the few vehicles of eternal early-risers. A dirty blue MINI Cooper parks beside the cart cabin. Perhaps it belongs to an employee or just a regular customer, but it's there every week. A twenty-something young man smokes a cigarette on his break in front of the store near the flower baskets. He makes eye contact and nods his "good morning," waving his cancer stick. He probably worked the night shift. Inventory is being stocked for the busy day ahead. There is a slow hum in the store filled with the soft sounds of a small team of morning people, comprised of a few shoppers and employees. It feels much different from the frenzy of 5 p.m. on a London weekday when hurried and distracted people are stopping to pick up a bottle of milk or a loaf of bread on their way home from work. It's now almost calming. Too early yet for the common man.

    The same faces are seen every week doing the same tasks in the same aisles. Politeness and respect are innate and float through the store amidst the sounds of cans being shelved, the high-pitched squeaks of a defective wheel on a shopping cart, or the whir of the coffee maker in the bakery area. There is soft music piping through the speaker. Chatter and laughter in

Finding Victoria

the seafood area can be heard as the display is loaded up with ice and prawns, fish of all varieties, and scallops. I go through each aisle, pausing in all the usual spots. My pen-scrawled shopping list rarely deviates from week to week. Organic veggies, skinless chicken breasts, cheese, bananas, berries, oat milk, and perhaps a few loaves of fresh bread among the other usual suspects. I am guaranteed a conversation with the produce man, Owen, who shares a bit of his life story as he fills the first vegetable tiers with celery, mushrooms, onions, and lettuce.

"I was once a farmer in these parts," he begins. "Family's been farming south of Liverpool for two hundred years." Carefully laying the carrots neatly, he adds, "But it's the dairies that fare the best..." He elaborates, and I pause among the spinach and tomatoes to listen.

I have heard him talk of the family farm many times over, but I look forward to his cheerful chatter and sincere smile as he continues his work and says with a wink, "Have yerself a lovely day, my love."

"And you," I return, and give a half-wave as I move on to the next aisle, list in hand and pen in the other.

The elderly man with the long white ponytail has arrived. He's a little late today. We never speak but always cordially exchange a nonverbal greeting: I salute him because I know he is a military veteran from his hat that reads, "Have you kissed a veteran today?" He always blows me a kiss. The man operates his mobile cart like he is ready to take it to a motocross competition. Part of the Sunday routine. Then he speeds off.

Hattie is at the end of Aisle 6 with the cheese showcase. She likes to have a small slice of cheese waiting for me on a napkin.

"Got your Stilton here today, Marie. How might you like a nice bit of Roquefort on the side? Aged to perfection, it is. Give it a try," she coaxes. Handing over the breakfast starters. She waits for my response.

Hattie's right. The creaminess dances on my taste buds, awakens the senses with its tanginess.

Finding Victoria

"I'll take some of the Roquefort, Hattie. Good call," and I estimate the slice size with a gesture of my fingers, measuring the air. "Perfect!" I watch her wrap it with great care and thank her.

Business as usual. Everyone is in their place. But the highlight of the Sainsbury's weekly shop has yet to arrive: little Angus McGregor.

There is no mistaking when Angus is in the store. The energy of the six-year-old is electric. The volume of voices increases as cries of "Good morning, Angus!" echo in every aisle.

"I'll be getting that treat for you, my boy," Henry the baker guarantees, peering down over the counter at the eager brown-haired boy with the thick-lensed glasses; Howard disappears and then reappears with something sweet for Angus.

"Come over here and let me have a look at you," remarks Hattie, "Why you must have grown ten inches since I last seen you!"

"When are you going to come work behind the counter with me, Angus?" asks Samuel, the butcher.

"Hand me that can of beans, Angus," points the stock boy, Rhys. "Make sure you get the cans on the bottom shelf there all lined up."

"Where's my hug, little man?" beckons Amelia, in the flower department with her arms wide open. She has all the marks of a loving grandmother.

Angus is a joyous store celebrity, complete with his quiet but proud bodyguard father, who just follows a few steps behind his young son with the empty cart. It's quite a Sunday outing. An event. And their social rounds to each department come before any actual shopping is started.

I witness this show of love every Sunday and have done so for months, mentioning it to my adult children from time to time. It has become the running joke in my family after a while.

They started regularly asking me, "Did you see Angus this week?" or "Maybe you should invite him to tea?" My son, in

Finding Victoria

particular, began to tease me by saying, "I think Angus is in your head," or "C'mon, mom, just admit it...there is no Angus."

But one morning, my daughter was visiting for the weekend, and she agreed to accompany me on my ritual Sunday morning trek to Sainsbury's after her required stop at the nearby Starbucks for her macchiato grande. And before I got through Aisle 2, there was Angus! As if on cue, he ran toward me to give me a hug. This had never happened before. He and I had only ever shared smiles. I was not yet part of the inner circle of the Angus McGregor Fan Club. I had always been just the quiet observer, the witness to weekly unblemished joy.

"Thank you," I whispered before releasing him. I was actually a little overcome with unexpected emotion.

My daughter laughed, and I said, "Angus, this is my daughter, Hannah. And Hannah, this is Angus!" The introduction solidified that I was not certifiable. My daughter smiled broadly at my secret triumph.

"Pleasure," she nodded at Angus, eager to confirm to my son that I was not losing it. Then the boy raced away, waving to both of us, heading off to the next stop on his weekly Sainsbury's goodwill tour.

Some months later, however, the boy and his father were absent from the store. One Sunday passed. And another. Silence shrouded the weekend mornings that were no longer the inspiration they had been. I had so enjoyed witnessing those interactions with Angus, but they were no more. Abruptly halted. The tenor changed. Although the employees were still courteous, the polish was gone. Angus was gone. No one spoke of him. And as Oscar Wilde said, "Nothing is permanent except change." Angus found other interests, no doubt. Or he moved. And that's that.

But this "Angus McGregor Effect" has never left me. The smallest opportunity to make eye contact, smile, and say "hello" to strangers in passing became a real mission in the years that followed. It felt good, even if people did not respond. It became

Finding Victoria

a game I played when out in public. How many people could I get to positively respond? I was trying to make connections, and that's what mattered. I got better and better at it. One man I saw regularly on my walks into town started beating me to the greeting. We laughed. We talked. In time, we became friends. We even fell in love.

Perhaps one day I will see Angus again, but if you see him before I do, be sure to give him a smile and hug for me, and tell him thank you!

Finding Victoria

Finding Victoria

3 The Digby Five

Luke Finn had never been much of an athlete, but it never mattered much to him. However, he did feel intimidated when he learned his four boarding school roommates were talented athletic runners. They were all on the Abington School track and field team as fifteen and sixteen-year-olds. It was 1985.

Abington was nestled on the edge of Exmoor National Park in the West Country between Minehead and Taunton. It attracted those from modest rural towns, but there were also the well-connected and wealthy who sent their sons (and now daughters) for an elite education. In the not-too-distant past, Abington's reputation had been plagued by rumors of sexual indecency and other horrors inflicted upon some of the students, but there had been many firings of staff and new rules instituted since then. Its dignified image reinstated, Abington stood as one of the premier schools in the United Kingdom, with a comparable sticker price.

Somehow, the dormitory was overbooked, and Luke ended up as the extra inhabitant of a room designated for four students, not five. But the school accommodated the situation as best it could by adding a bunk bed and deducting some cost from the boarding bill. Luke was grateful, and his new roommates were welcoming. They made it work.

Finding Victoria

Luke recalled when he first arrived at Room 514 in Digby Hall. There were small shards of hay on the back of his trousers.

"Just get off the farm?" chuckled Ben, who arrived early; he was folding a few items and tucked them into a drawer as he surveyed the newcomer. He barely looked up at Luke but made a quick and accurate assessment.

"Uh, yes, quite right…Devon," Luke smiled shyly, "I'm Luke."

"Ben," he held a polite hand out, and then teased, "You know you will be expected to run the mile in under five if you are going to stay in this room! You are in lightning-fast company!"

"What?" the farm boy uttered with a panicked tone but then realized it was a joke. "Oh, yeah, I'm not an athlete."

"That's pretty clear," Ben stroked his newly acquired blond peach-fuzz mustache and took a hard look at the new arrival. "I'm taking the top bunk, if you don't mind. The rest are up to you until the others get here. Ah, speak of the devils…"

Two boys, saddled with duffle bags and schoolbooks, stood in the doorway. Will, a lanky lad with thick brown hair, stood almost six inches taller than Tom, who was more muscular and compact in stature.

"What have we got here?" smirked Tom, dropping his bags with a thump. "I sure as hell am not bunking," he added, pointing to the double-decker against the wall.

"I got that one, mate. I like to be on top," Ben confirmed.

"That's what we hear. Your mum told me so," teased Will, flashing a bright smile.

"Your sister will tell you that, too!" Ben shot back in jest. "This here's Luke…straight from the chicken coops of Devon! Luke, meet the girls: Will and Tom."

Everyone exchanged nods of introduction, and then Tom seemed to emerge as the outspoken leader of the group. He outlined the procedures of the dining hall, laundry facilities, and other schedules. He was a veteran among them at sixteen, but it was clear to Luke that the trio were familiar with each other, likely through training and competitions, as well as their prior residence at Abingdon. They unloaded their things, each claiming a slice of space in the spartan room.

"Where's that rascal Hamish?" Ben posed. "He still owes me forty quid from the entry fee for that marathon in Glasgow last month."

"That the one he dodged because it went through the necropolis?" smiled Will, but conceded, "Tough race."

"Yes, but he was having ankle issues. Those hills would have destroyed him…" admitted Ben, "…outside of his ghost fear."

"You run at all, Luke?' Tom seriously inquired.

"No. The family has a dairy farm. I'm here to be an accountant. Trying to keep the business end of things afloat for my father."

"Well, we'll make a runner of you yet," promised Tom as he ran a comb through his wavy, strawberry-blond hair in front of the timid mirror.

"Look at you. Primping for the ladies already!" joked Ben.

"The world's my oyster, boys!" Tom winked.

"Not much chance of seeing many of those for a while. Don't waste your time," commented Will. "Let's go get some lunch," he suggested; he was forever hungry. "Hamish can catch up with us later. Luke, prepare yourself for a feast of slop with a side of chips!"

The four filed out amidst more playful taunting and debauchery.

Rural life was all Luke had known. And having no siblings put him at a distinct disadvantage in this camaraderie of testosterone, clever witticism, and fitness. But he was game, and he knew that his own advantages and strengths would present themselves. For now, his reticence served him well, and these newfound friends respected him for his differences in perspective. They were a jolly group.

But it was ironically Hamish who seemed the proverbial

third wheel, or fifth, in this case. He arrived later that evening a bit harried and moody.

"Hamish! At last!" greeted Tom, who had settled into his running journal, reviewing recent times for his recorded distances. He chronicled every pace, every step, and every weather condition for his runs. Meticulous.

Hamish surveyed the room, realizing there were to be five inhabitants instead of the typical four. Luke felt targeted when Hamish sternly commented, "What charity case is this?" gesturing with a head nod toward Luke.

"Abingdon is cutting our board costs for taking Luke here in. Didn't you get the letter? Too many students this semester. We're not going to be here much between classes and practices. At least we have the larger room. Don't get your knickers in a twist," assured Tom.

"Yeah, yeah, okay," Hamish tossed his bags upon the remaining empty bed. "Anyone have food? I'm famished. The train was held up three times on the way. Thought I'd never get here," Hamish groused. He had the body of a shot-putter, but he ran a wicked half-marathon.

Luke offered some scones and biscuits his mother had packed for him. "Help yourself," as he held out the tired tin.

"Thanks," Hamish grabbed several things from the tin without making eye contact and collapsed on the bed. "What time is practice in the morning?" he asked the room.

"Seven at Derby Park. Distancers are doing a five-mile loop for time. Will, the hurdlers don't need to show up until eight at the fieldhouse. Is that right?" asked Tom.

"That's right," Will confirmed.

Luke had surmised Tom and Hamish were the distance runners; Will and Ben were the hurdlers and sprinters.

"Looks like YOU get to have a lie-in tomorrow, Farm Boy!" chirped Ben.

"Mmmm...no, class at eight," corrected Luke, who was looking forward to getting his academic routines in order.

Finding Victoria

"I will see you all for lunch?

"Save a few chairs, whoever gets there first," Will suggested, and then turned over to sleep.

A fairly uneventful first day, Luke decided, but he was curious about Hamish. In the days ahead, his story would unfold.

Lunches became the daily meeting of the minds and antics filled with teenagers who still had the maturity of eleven-year-old boys. The interactions all seemed a bit like *Dead Poet Society* without the venerable Mr. Keating and without much intellectual conversation. But Luke felt like he had been accepted into the distinctive society of Digby Hall, more importantly, Room 514.

A notable tradition began that semester led by Ben, where the very large bulletin board on the fifth floor of Digby Hall became the center of artistic expression for the building. The Picassos, led by Room 514, periodically smuggled out random food from the dining hall and made fresh abstract additions to the almost fresco-like blank canvas of the board: smears of ketchup, textured splotches of mashed potatoes, vegetable soup broth, and an array of unidentifiables. Hamish was able to adhere several strands of fettuccine in a corner where it became petrified and admired. Even an apprehensive Luke participated in the crude activity. His proud contribution was a message with alphabet soup letters spelling out "GOD WAS HERE," and it stayed intact, glued for three congealed weeks until the final "E" fell off (or was tampered with) to state "GOD WAS HER" to the delight of the few occasional female witnesses. The visitor traffic to the fifth floor increased to view the famed spectacle. Abstract art at its best. But no one of any authoritative consequence ever saw it, so the menagerie of victuals remained. It would have been an instant social media sensation if cell phones had been in use. But, alas, it would survive only in the memory of the hall's residents.

The Digby Five, as the rabble-rouser group became known, were the inciters of other mischievous incidents on school grounds. Luke became the ringleader for the infamous UNO tournaments in the basement of the hall. His financial acumen was put to use in organizing the gambling events almost in "flash mob" style, but without the internet. Word-of-mouth was just as effective. The quiet farm boy had come out of his shell. The revenue was incredible. There was even one professor, Mr. Munroe, who participated until a student foolishly mentioned it in class in front of the dean. Mr. Munroe quietly disappeared into the stratosphere of ethically challenged instructors.

When the December holiday break came, it was a welcome respite from not only classes and track practices but from the tireless energy expended on the inappropriate social events the Digby Five carried out.

Hamish was the last to leave the hall. His father was late arriving.

"Catch a ride with me to Taunton," offered Luke. "Your father won't have to drive as far. Go give him a call before they lock the dorms up later."

"It's fine," lied Hamish. "My father's probably stuck at the hospital." This had been a slip; he did not try to recover.

"Oh, why is he there?" asked a surprised Luke. It was a rarity when Hamish got personal, and he never spoke of home.

"Uh, me mum's been sick. The big C. It won't be long now." Silence.

"Sorry, man. I didn't know."

"No one knows."

Luke put a hand on Hamish's shoulder in support and then wished him well before walking toward his ride. Those three words haunted him as he watched Hamish in the distance. "No one knows." What do any of us really know about each other? It was sad truth.

Hamish returned from the break more silent and brooding than ever, but only Luke noticed; however, he didn't ask his quiet roommate any questions. He appeared to be the same old Hamish to everyone else, gruff and complaining. Gloom and doom. In contrast, the popularity on campus of the Digby Five soared that spring, not only due to the rogueries, but the track and field team was winning and a contender for the championship. Will had set records, Tom became the celebrated captain, and Ben surpassed his personal bests. Hamish, however, was relegated to the bench for most of the spring season; he was struggling in more ways than one. Luke attended the meets when he could to support his now very popular roommates.

Ben turned up one afternoon with a critter he named Scruffy. It was a white hamster with flecks of black on its back.

"What the hell? You can't keep that here," Hamish told him.

"Sure, we can; who's going to know?" argued Ben.

Will asked to hold him. "Hand him over. What do these fellows eat?"

"Your fingers, idiot!" said Tom.

"We need a cage or something," Luke suggested. "Ben's right. Who will know?"

And it was surprisingly Hamish who got the cage.

For several weeks, Scruffy thrived. It became an instant attraction when girls were invited and covertly brought to the room. Food was easy enough to get from the dining hall, so it was reasonably easy and inexpensive to keep Scruffy as a pet. No escape mishaps and minimal clean-up. He was well-fed.

It was Hamish who discovered Scruffy's lifeless and stiff body. The team had just won the championship, and he was the first to return to the room. The wet uniform clung to him, having been recently baptized in orange Gatorade.

Luke then entered the main part of the room to see Hamish crouching over the cage. A tear splashed from his cheek, but he quickly wiped it away and looked up at his farm boy friend.

"Hey, man," started Luke.

"Hey," as Hamish stood up. "Damn rodent kicked the bucket."

While Luke was surprised by this revelation, he considered the half-assed care the creature received and decided he had

Finding Victoria

lived a lengthy life under such conditions.

"What should we do with him?"

"It belongs to Ben. He can decide," and he closed the cage door. Then Hamish said, "My mother died this afternoon. I just called my father to tell him about the team. She died."

The others suddenly bounded in, whooping and singing Queen's "We Are the Champions," and Will tripped over his own jacket when they came through the door, knocking over Tom, followed by laughter. They collapsed into a riotous pile.

"Scruffy died," Luke stated. He watched Hamish leave the room.

"How did that happen?" asked Ben, seemingly little concerned.

"He probably exploded from eating too much. All he does is eat. We should've got 'im a hamster wheel," replied Tom, who picked himself up off the floor and went to the cage.

"We'll have a proper Viking funeral for him in the morning," said Ben. "Just before sunrise. River Exe. Near the docks."

The mood had turned, and the celebration eased.

"Great night, boys," Luke commended, trying to divert the emotion prompted by the death. "You all deserve to celebrate."

A sensitive Will now offered, "We'll toast the win tomorrow night. I'm knackered. Going to hit the sheets."

"Yeah, sounds good," said Tom, who walked off to the bathroom for a shower.

Ben placed a t-shirt over the cage out of respect.

"Goodnight, boys! Helluva night! And a good night to you too, Scruffy!"

Luke was concerned about Hamish and did not sleep until he heard him return in the middle of the night. But no words were exchanged.

The following morning, the preparations were made. Ben disappeared while it was still dark, gathering twigs and other materials to construct the pyre. Will rummaged through the desk drawers for a bit of string and a lighter.

Finding Victoria

Hamish emerged from his room, entering the common area. "What's going on? Don't you guys sleep?"

"We're having a funeral for Scruffy," stated Will, "Aha, this lighter works!" He flicked it several times until the flame jumped out.

There was no time to make this a public event, even though it would have been quite something! Luke imagined students lining the parking lot to pay respects to Scruffy. There would be flowers, music, and candles could be sold. But it was private. Personal. A dark comedy. A Viking funeral for a hamster.

The quintet dressed formally, complete with tie and suit jacket, but with sandals and sneakers to walk along the riverbank where they would launch the rodent to the great beyond. The procession was led by Ben, who carried the cage. He was followed by Will, with the raft and kindling. Tom and Luke thoughtfully plucked a few wildflowers along the path with Hamish trailing in the rear, hands in pockets.

The pyre was mounded on the small makeshift raft, Scruffy placed on top, and small flowers laid as Will flicked the lighter.

"We need to do a prayer first," said Tom, half-smirking, but wanting to maintain the serious but ironic tone.

"Ben, you should do it," suggested Luke.

"Okay," agreed Ben and then surprised them all with a small sheet of notes he had composed very early that morning. The paper was rumpled as he pulled it out of his coat pocket.

"Today, we humbly meet to say goodbye to our dear friend, Scruffy," he began. "He was a good and loyal roommate. He wasn't always the tidiest, but he gave us great joy in the company of girls, for which we are very appreciative."

Will poked Tom, as they tried to suppress their laughter. They both knew it was only Tom who used the hamster as a pick-up line to lure girls to the room. One girl screamed when she realized there was a live rodent next to her on the couch.

Ben continued, "Death does not need to be the end. We have our memories to sustain us. We will cherish the memory of

Finding Victoria

Scruffy's muddy footprints all over the bathroom floor, his droppings left on our desks, and the shredded lettuce he hoarded under our beds..."

Hamish stopped listening to Ben after "memories to sustain us." He was recalling his own memories, those of his mother. She had been ill for so long; he was not sure if he felt relieved because she was not suffering any longer or because he did not have to worry and wonder when the end would finally come. Luke glanced over at Hamish compassionately and lowered his head to acknowledge him, and the silent pain he was dealing with.

"And so now, we commit the body of Scruffy to the heavenly domain of the afterlife, where he will chew through endless boxes and paper and will enjoy running on his spiritual hamster wheel forever. Rest in peace, Scruffy."

Will brought the lighter to the pyre and shielded the wind from its flame and from Scruffy.

"Wait!" commanded Hamish. He took a small bookmark and placed it on the raft at the base of the mound. He was stoic.

It had been a gift from his mother, inscribed in her own handwriting with words of encouragement: "True strength is cultivated quietly when the storms, floods, and winds swirl all around us."

No one knew what the bookmark said, and no one had questioned the gesture. But Luke had seen the bookmark previously on Hamish's desk. He never forgot those words. He had a whole new respect for his friend, Hamish. A person of quiet strength.

The Digby Five watched the beautiful flames glide down the river.

Finding Victoria

4 How Gordon Ramsay Saved My Marriage

My flagrant flaw: I am an American…married to a Brit. The former part is the flaw here, not the latter. At least to my husband.

Amid an uncomfortable marital separation, being American suddenly meant I had the plague, even though it was a superpower when we were happily in the depths of our courtship. Driving on the left side of the road became a skill deficiency, even though the elderly local town driving instructor, Raleigh, had done his best to encourage my skills with repeated comments like "A little to the right, a little to the right," and "Slow it down on the bend." Full disclosure, Raleigh had a reputation for womanizing and only taking on female clients.

Where politics were reasonably well tolerated throughout our relationship in the past, now, any support on my part for American leadership was a catalyst for an argument. I could not win in a country of monarchs that in the 1700s had prompted my ancestors to pack up and leave! A point we used to laugh about, but not anymore.

I used to have the Midas touch when it came to any topic discussed between us, only now, every subject I touched on seemed to turn to shit.

I was not even certain when exactly the relationship fell apart.

Finding Victoria

It was like my husband, George, woke up one morning and decided Americans are the enemy, and I became the helpless collateral damage. Things seemed stale. I moved out of our quaint British bungalow and found a temporary flat in town until any final decisions were to be made. A separation might be good. In the meantime, we were going to try counseling. I was still reeling over the suddenness of it.

"Marriages are complicated" has to be the biggest understatement of all time. George and I had no children, but we could boast a twenty-five-year marriage. We spent the early years of wedded bliss in the United States when business was profitable for George. He was a salesman for a pharmaceuticals company on the East Coast, even though he would have been so much more content and thriving with a job that put him in the thick of nature and among living creatures: farmer, gamekeeper, beekeeper, dog groomer, etc., I would hate to see the statistics on how many people there are who actually enjoy and are passionate about the occupation they hold. My guess is not many George was most definitely among this group. My career changes have been many: from nanny to waitress to secretary, and even hospice manager. I was now forty-nine and still trying to decide what I wanted to be when I grew up. However, we lived comfortably and traveled the world. We were happy, "were" being the operative word.

But when business soured in 2023, we decided to change rail tracks, and moved back to the United Kingdom. And although I felt the familial tug to remain in the country where my aging parents, siblings, and many nieces and nephews lived, I knew it was time to put myself first and follow my husband's lead. Marriage is about negotiation and sacrifice. George had put in his time in America; now it was my turn. Point for George. But who is keeping score?

When we went to the marriage counselor for the first time, I was unrealistically expecting solutions to problems. Instead, it was questions.

Finding Victoria

"Why are you here?" she initiated with my husband.

A woman, in her mid-fifties, her face was worn with the minutes and hours of absorbing negative energy from countless couples who came in with only the facade of an intent to fix their relationship. The hypocrisy of it stained the walls of her office. But there was also a hopefulness in her demeanor, and her bright blue eyes gleamed when she did, on occasion, smile. She adjusted her glasses a little tighter to her face and seemed to study my husband's response with particular interest. She reminded me of the therapist from *The Sopranos*. I even noticed George give her the up and down. He was always studying women, which did not bother me. I found it amusing how blatantly obvious he was. Looking was the extent of his admiration, and it wasn't always a sexual thing. Or maybe it was?

I, too, turned in my chair, seated next to him, to get a better sense of what his response would be. "Because my wife made me," echoed quietly in my head.

"I want to save my marriage. I love my wife," he calmly said. He reached for my hand.

And why are you here?" the cautious counselor turned to me.

I paused…too long. I was trying too hard to come up with what would be perceived as the "right" answer, a hopeful outlook. Instead, it seemed like I didn't care.

I could peripherally see my husband's shoulder slump a bit in dejection over my hesitation. Oh, God…wrong reaction, I thought.

"I…I… want us to be happy again," I blurted.

"Aren't you happy?" the counselor posed.

"She's just distant, uninterested…in me," calmly interjected George. He did not look at me as he said this.

"No! That's not it!" I protested. "It's the stress. I feel like a fish out of water since moving to the UK. I don't have a say in things. I am a stranger in my own home. I'm still adjusting since the move."

"She's too American." He denounced out loud to this

stranger. I laughed, nervously, unsure of what he meant.

"What have you done to help her feel better about this move?" the counselor asked.

"Well, I've had the gardener plant the flowers she loves. I have hired a cook to help with meals, so she has more time to focus on herself. I've brought in a cleaner too."

"I sometimes feel trapped. I can't even drive myself anywhere!" I whined.

"You've had the lessons," he reminded her.

"Three lessons. I'd be happier with an automatic," she confessed. "It would make a big difference. I've said that before. No one drives a stick-shift in the States. It's hard enough I have to drive on the left side of the road. Cut me a little slack here."

"It's a nightmare being in a car with you," he accused in a non-maliciously intended manner, "Not to mention the fear factor when you enter a roundabout!" He was clearly agitated.

"But I've only driven a handful of times. Give me some credit! I need more practice. I'll take more lessons!"

The counselor quickly tapped at her laptop, and then she looked up at my husband and changed the subject. "Let's redirect for a minute. Have you told her you feel neglected? How have you made this known?"

"She pushes the envelope when it comes to limitations on *things*," he emphasized the last word. I knew that meant intimacy and affection. "I've been very patient with this mid-life stress she puts on everything. I miss the laughter and her attention. There's no spontaneity. I get more attention from the woman at the grocery store checkout. She knows; I've said it a dozen times," he added.

I stewed a bit in my seat and shifted uncomfortably. The physical attraction I had to my husband was never in question. I have never been more attracted to any other man…ever. In that department, I felt we were made for each other, but perhaps he was right; I needed to focus more on him instead of the unnecessary worries I created. Point for him.

Finding Victoria

"Hmmm...." More tapping on the keyboard. "You have both insisted you have voiced your feelings with each other, but that is not what I am sensing. Communication happens in many ways. It seems like neither one of you is doing an effective job on this. You are both too afraid of hurting the other, but you are, in essence, making a mess of it all by not speaking up honestly. Are you familiar with the term 'conflict-avoidant'?"

We both shook our heads.

That seemed like a canned analysis, but it turned out to be the truth. George and I spent so much time insulating each other's feelings that real honesty had escaped us. Things festered. We were caught in a spiral of guessing games and frustration that usually erupted in hurt feelings, always kind of floating above the surface with molten lava boiling beneath.

The counselor was careful to balance the continued questions between us both for the remainder of the session. And I was caught off-guard with a few comments George made, but I stubbornly knew he was correct in his analysis of what was going on in my head. I had become too preoccupied with making things perfect, and when I couldn't accomplish that, it created unnecessary stress. I had become withdrawn, but not intentionally. He, on the other hand, seemed to take me for granted. There was the expectation I would just fall in line with his whims and routines. He did not like controversy. Maybe we were conflict-avoidant? He was the leader and I the follower, most times. Living in the UK seemed to give him an unfair home advantage. I liked the way we lived, but I wanted some kind of recognition, I suppose. Some sense of belonging. Ultimately, we both wanted similar things. We both wanted and needed a reset, but we didn't know how to go about it.

However, a breakdown in a relationship is rarely one-sided, so when he said, "We have nothing in common anymore," my jaw must have dropped. Another can of worms to tackle.

"Where was all this coming from?" I thought. You don't stay with someone this long if there aren't things in common...do

Finding Victoria

you? After twenty-five years?

More clicking on the keyboard.

The session continued with civil discourse, but the enlightenment that occurred in that small office was earth-shattering to me. And the disquiet was something we both felt. The depth of the truth surged like a tidal wave.

"Here's what I propose for your homework…" Dr. Hargreaves said to lighten the mood. "I want you both to host a dinner party for at least six guests. The theme is Gordon Ramsay, and it can be implemented however you like. You must make this a joint endeavor. Report back to me at the next session in two weeks."

"Are you serious?" I asked, but oddly open to the idea.

"Quite."

George and I exchanged glances. He sparked up; I rolled my eyes.

We left the office bewildered.

"So, what are we going to do?" my husband looked at me; he seemed oddly open to this idea.

"Jeez, I don't know. Maybe we should watch a few episodes of *Kitchen Nightmares*?" I was quite serious.

To be clear, I was very nervous about this proposal for a dinner party. It was foolish, but it's how I felt.

We settled in a market town in Wiltshire, the county that held the bragging rights as the home of Stonehenge. There was a cultural learning curve for me when we moved, even though I had spent much time in the UK in the early days of our marriage, either while traveling or visiting with my husband's friends and family. When we first moved to the house on the outskirts of the village, my husband wanted to celebrate by inviting some friends to dinner. I hardly knew where all of the pots and pans were at that point, with boxes still unopened from the move.

Admittedly, I have never perfected the British dinner party. Even that phrase "dinner party" seems like something straight

Finding Victoria

out of the 1960s to me. But it's a serious thing across the pond. The American version is that you invite an assortment of your friends to dinner. In the summer months, it consists of grilling, there's a nearby cooler full of ice and drinks, with harder cocktails on the kitchen counter, a help-yourself buffet of dishes on the kitchen table, and accoutrements such as the standard condiment caddy, plasticware, paper plates, paper napkins, etc. No Spode china or Waterford crystal here.

I need a manual to execute the British dinner party. But in fairness to my friends in the land of Queen Elizabeth and King Charles, there is something very special and delightful about the protocol and tradition. I am just so damn intimidated by it as an American hostess. It applies quite a bit of pressure and jacks up the stakes, especially when you are someone like me who has relatively average cooking skills, and even more average knowledge of solid British fare. Fish and chips, maybe? Shepherd's pie, lamb tagine, or even a decent curry do not come easily.

We had a gas stove, which I had never really cooked on before, at least no serious meals. Even making the necessary calculations to convert temperature degrees from Celsius to Fahrenheit was foreign to me. And it took me a while to determine that the British definition of "broil," which is definitely not the same thing as the American interpretation. Who could imagine that British and American English could be more different? Brits use the term "grill" in a different way, so, when my husband tells me to grill the steak, he means put it in the oven on high heat, not set up the patio grill for a barbecue. And this is just the food prep.

Setting the table is an ordeal, but one activity my husband actively takes part in. Before invitations go out, there is a concerted effort to be sure the proper number of genders are invited to keep the flow of an alternating seating pattern: male-female-male-female, etc. So, if you are single, do not be discouraged if you are not often invited to dinner; your host

Finding Victoria

must be having a challenging time finding the opposite gender guest to balance the table. Either that, or you may be sincerely unpopular! Throw in the proper place settings with the utensils, dishes, and glassware. Thank goodness for the internet and George. I think I may have learned how to set a table when I was a young kid in Girl Scouts, and since forgotten.

I mention these things, not as a complaint, but as significant details in the later litany of criticisms my husband made of my American ways. It was cute when we started dating. Later, it was an aggravation after he woke up on the wrong side of the bed. Was it something to divorce over? I was a product of my environment; no one taught me how to cook, and I was raised in a modest middle-class household with no formal dinner parties. I came upon this culinary ignorance honestly. However, I had never really made a conscious effort to get a better grasp of being the ultimate hostess either. Dinner parties scared the hell out of me. Me, 1 point; George, 1 point.

After we left the office of Dr. Hargreaves, George and I made a date to meet at the house. That evening, we sat on the sofa together. I came armed with a pad of paper and a bottle of merlot.

"You're taking notes?" George smirked, "Really?"

"Well, yes," I said resolutely.

"I think I could use some beer for this. Anything for you?"

"Um, yes, thank you. I'll take a small glass of that rosé that's opened in the fridge. And since when do you drink rosé?"

He handed the glass to me without answering the question,

"Here you go, Babe." I did not ask again.

"Babe"— I had not been called that in ages. But it was said more out of habit than any endearing signal.

I noticed he had not vacuumed recently and wanted to make a sarcastic comment but decided to bite my tongue. It would help nothing. What did it matter anyhow?

"Oh, God, this restaurant is a PIT!" I cried with giggles as Gordon Ramsay walked onscreen and did his usual harsh critique of the establishment and the menu items. Ramsay rifled through the walk-in freezer, castigating spoiled meat, rancid sauces, and even gagging at the smell of soured food. I bubbled with more laughter.

George grinned at the sound of my sincere joy. He seemed more amused by me than any of Ramsay's onslaught of expletives.

By the end of three episodes, my notepad was full, and George and I were leaning into each other on the couch, prompted by drowsiness. I missed this. It was too natural.

My husband took the empty glasses and rinsed them in the kitchen. "I think we're off to a fair start." I nodded as I followed him into the kitchen. "Take that merlot. You never drank it."

"I'll get my coat. Meet you in the morning?" I suggested.

"Follow up with breakfast at The Nook? How does nine sound?" he proposed. His recent job allowed him flex time since he was working remotely.

"That's a little late for you, isn't it?" This detail had my attention. George was an early-bird riser and as regular as the changing of the guard at Buckingham Palace.

"A little. Trying to put some things together for work. I need to walk the dog, too."

"Okay, then," I let myself out and called, "See you in the morning. I'll bring my notes!"

The Nook was crowded even for nine o'clock. We sat outside and plotted our strategy for the dinner event, and I reviewed my notes from *Kitchen Nightmares*.

We recited the mantras of Ramsay.

"No microwaved food!" I cried.

"Simple menu," Ralph added after sipping his flat white.

"Fresh ingredients. I can get those at the farmer's market on Wednesday. We'll do the dinner on Thursday."

"Mmmmm…I have plans for Thursday," he said with some uncertainty, and paused, "But I can probably change them. Thursday it is."

Finding Victoria

"Okay. Who do you want to invite? We can do eight."

"Definitely Andrew and Celia. Celia knows Paul's wife, so we could also ask Paul and Mary?" These were all nearby neighbors.

"I am okay with that. Can we ask Trudy? I haven't seen her in town for a while. Got any thoughts on who to pair her with?"

"Trudy?" George's expression exhibited some apprehension. "I don't think Celia cares much for Trudy." He rubbed his forehead.

"Oh, it's fine. There will be enough people. We need a single for Trudy, then. How about Andy Richards? He's single again, right? Too blue blood for this gathering?" I asked.

"No, Richards will work. I just hope he doesn't engage in his usual name-dropping," George rolled his eyes.

"I'll handle the invites, and you decide on the menu."

People passed in and out of the café and took special note that George and I were "together" despite the recognized separation we had instituted. Small towns are funny that way. People notice everything, but they rarely interpret things with much accuracy. Who knows what they were thinking as they curiously watched us? And then, almost as if on cue, Trudy, with her cocker spaniel, turned the corner.

We knew Trudy from some church socials. She appeared a little surprised to see us; she knew of our recent separation. Despite her muddied wellies, oversized coat, and graying light brown hair pulled back with a bandana; I watched George give her the signature up and down. While I was not very jealous, I was a little irritated. I suppose my feathers were ruffled…a bit.

"Oh, nice to see you George… Rachael," she paused as her dog, Ruffles, vigorously sniffed the ground near my chair. No doubt he was discovering the crumbs of breakfast.

"Trudy," nodded George in acknowledgement. "How are things at the shop?"

She had a small boutique at the top of the hill where she sold perfumes, lotions, handmade soaps, and other feminine delights.

"Oh, fine, fine. I have a shipment of things coming in from

Finding Victoria

Manchester this afternoon. Rachael, you might want to stop in next week after I have shelved everything. There are some beautiful handmade sweaters I think you would like," Trudy shared, tugging authoritatively on Ruffles' lead as her dog wanted desperately to chase after a passing beagle. "George, I guess I'll see you on the path with the dog later. Good day to both of you," and she hurried away.

It was not uncommon for George to meet up with folks on the meadow trails as he walked our collie, Blarney. But, there was something about Trudy's comment that made it seem like this meeting with the dogs was part of a routine now.

I wanted to make a sarcastic remark but refrained. We were trying to sort out our marriage. That would not be beneficial in any way. They say the wife is the last to know. Was I being ridiculously suspicious and sensitive? But George's mind had already moved on from the brief encounter and was back to Gordon Ramsay.

"I would like a prawn cocktail to start things off, followed by Beef Wellington with vegetables," George announced with conviction, "And how about a nice sticky toffee pudding?"

"Tall order, but I think that's good," I commended the choices.

"Okay, I must run," said George, anxiously looking at his watch. "I'll sort out the seating arrangements later once we get the invite confirmations."

"I'll do the shopping, and let's talk again Wednesday night," I said, as an offering of sincere effort.

"Why don't we just do the shopping together?"

"Well, okay, if you want." I was honestly a little surprised.

"I'll ring you," as he rushed off and disappeared around the corner, leaving a fiver and some coins tossed haphazardly on the table.

Maybe we did not need this assignment from the therapist? I thought. Things had been reasonable between us in the last twenty-four hours.

Finding Victoria

The afternoon leading up to the dinner party presented many challenges, not unexpected. George had rearranged the cabinets a little since I moved out, so finding pots and pans created a cacophony of banging and crashing. George gave me a hard, scolding expression over the noise.

"Sorry," I said meekly. "You've moved things."

"Yes, just tell me what you are looking for," he dialed down the condescension.

"I see you are a step ahead of the Ramsay code for a clean kitchen environment," I complimented, opening the refrigerator, examining the contents. "Everything in its place."

I started chopping up vegetables with slices of carrot occasionally flying off the cutting board and onto the floor. I glanced at George for some critical reaction.

"We don't need veggie cannons," he laughed, picking up a few stray carrots from the floor. "Shall I season the beef?"

That sounded like a sexual reference, and I giggled like a juvenile.

The kitchen was relatively small, so as he reached around me for the meat pan, I was keenly aware of his arm around my waist and his cheek near mine. God, I missed that. His sandalwood scent washed over me.

"Sure. Season the beef…that sounds dirty," I smiled, testing the waters a bit. He had ignored the sexual innuendo.

"When you're done with that, can you set the table? Not my strength," I said.

"Yes, I know," but it was with a lighter tone, and not one of accusation. He busied himself with his task.

I admired his sense of protocol and order. But when it came time for the napkins, we discovered the only ones in the house were a handful of hodgepodge misfit paper ones with "Over the Hill," printed on some, others with bright watermelons, and two crumpled ones with "Happy New Year!" blazed across them.

"Oh, God!" I laughed in humorous horror. "Let me run over to the store and get something appropriate. Presentation is everything, right?"

"I'll go," he offered. "You don't want to use the morbid 'Over the Hill' ones?" I think he was half serious, and for a minute, I wanted to go along with the suggestion just to see the reaction of our guests.

There was a playfulness in our preparations that I had not felt in a long time. I wanted to kiss him. And I think he wanted to kiss me, too. The afternoon carried on in this manner, and despite a few mishaps, we successfully shared a moment…a kitchen moment, but nonetheless, it seemed a minor relationship turning point in our ability to get along. I felt a shift. Maybe.

The doorbell rang. Guests arrived. George served the drinks, and I laid out the nibbles. I thought about Ramsay and where things usually go horribly wrong when food gets served, and I waited for the other shoe to drop as the evening wore on. The meat might be too dry, too salty, or too undercooked, as was so often the case in Ramsay's critiques. The courses could have been grossly mistimed. But that never happened. George and I shared premature, passive congratulatory looks at each other across the ends of the table. He was not viewing me as an "American" now, but as a partner.

However, it was halfway through dinner when I took note that Trudy was fawning over the conversation with George, who was seated next to her. Short of sitting on his lap, there were too many casual touches as she grabbed his wrist at one point, poked his shoulder, and even patted his cheek. He reveled in the attention. While Paul and Andrew, who flanked me, discussed the stock market and their investments, I tried to stay engaged, with one eye on my flirting husband.

"What do you think about cryptocurrency, Rachael?" Andrew asked me. "This beef is wonderful!" he added.

"Uh, I don't know a thing about it," I laughed. "Give me good old American stocks and I am happy." I looked at the other end of the table.

The curtain was pulled back. I understood what he yearned

Finding Victoria

For in that moment. George caught my glance and realized I had clarity. It was Trudy. And whether anything had ever physically transpired between them, I did not want to know. She was interested. George was separated from me and entitled. But as we cleared the dishes later, after everyone left, I came up behind him at the sink and territorially wrapped my arms tightly around him, kissing him on the back of the neck, then laying my cheek on the back of his shoulder in a familiar way.

"The evening was a success!" exclaimed George, almost in disbelief but not acknowledging my affectionate advance.

"Can I meet you to walk Blarney tomorrow? I have some free time in the afternoon. Maybe we can talk some more about tonight and our next session with Dr. Hargreaves?"

He seemed a little surprised, but then, "Well, okay. Be here about 2 p.m.?"

And then I took a risk. "How about some extra dessert?" I seductively offered with my arms still about him.

He continued scrubbing the dishes. Silence. I withdrew. Rejection.

But then he turned, grinning. He instinctively wrapped his sudsy hands around my waist and kissed me passionately, which I was not convinced would happen, but I welcomed it. But then he pulled away just as suddenly as if stung by a wasp. It felt like a goodbye. Later, he told me that Trudy was just a superficial encounter at first, but that he wanted to explore his options. She was on the menu; I was off temporarily, but he missed me.

From that moment on, I referred to that night as our own little kitchen nightmare, or rather mine. You don't have to be a chef to recognize when the ingredients in a dish just aren't right and something is off. But, it can usually be remedied…a little extra spice, altering the ingredients just a bit. I wanted my husband back…from Trudy or whomever. He seemed to like the menu I once offered. And sometimes the quickest way to a man's heart is through the stomach, but through other means too. That experiment taught us both a few things.

Finding Victoria

We continued our counseling, even though the dinner party seemed a success. I was eager to piece our relationship back together, but it took almost a year and hard work.

"You're my comfort food," he told me later when we laughed about the dinner party and the counseling.

"And you're mine," I returned with a loving kiss on the cheek.

And that's how Gordon Ramsay saved my marriage…

Finding Victoria

Finding Victoria

5 Bunny Magic

Bunny Cranston was magic. You know the type of person where everything always seems to work out for them? Cranston's childhood friend, Dominic Covington, had witnessed it thousands of times over the decades. Tragedies avoided by mere inches, failures dodged at the last minute, and being in the right place at the right time. It was either magic or a guardian angel that was perpetually at her side. Dom coined it: "Bunny Magic."

When Bunny was one-tenth of a point short of having the highest grade point average for graduation, the guidance counselors recalculated the numbers and discovered an error that soon established her as valedictorian. She then had the honor of giving the speech. At age twenty-four, she needed her appendix removed. While in the hospital, Princess Diana made rounds on a charitable visitation and spoke to her. They talked mostly about what Bunny wanted to do with her life and her job hunt in the real estate business. They took a picture together, which Bunny treasured. But the brief interaction was far from superficial, because one month later, Sir Charles Spencer (Lady Di's brother) contacted her with some job leads in the city that eventually led to a very lucrative position. It was unbelievable.

Dom had always teased her that if it had been true Bunny Magic, she would have been married to Earl Spencer and would

Finding Victoria

have become a proper Lady. This always made her laugh. However, she sold her first house to the man who would become her husband, Gordon Reginald. And although not nobility, he was among the elite stockbrokers for the monarchy.

The magic sometimes presented itself in small ways, too. Walking into a shoe store and finding the perfect boots on sale, where her size was not there, but then the new shipment arrived just as she was leaving, and they had her size after all. Ordering takeaway, getting extra entrees in the order, and then being told she did not have to pay for the error. Getting a flat tire on a remote road (this is before cell phones), a friend happened to be driving by and gave her a ride. Being given a hospital-hosted party for the birth of her first child; her daughter, Christine, who was the 5000th infant to be born there. The list goes on of fortunate happenstances…Bunny Magic.

Dom first met Bunny in a London park at age nine, where squealing children ruled the day, and weary parents sat on wooden benches either showcasing their pride and bragging about their children's accomplishments or complaining of the difficulties of parenthood. Bunny's mother was the former, and Dom's father the latter.

Mrs. Cranston would often bring along a bag of bread bits to the park to feed the birds. "I don't know where these children get their energy," as she tossed the birds' next snack.

"Afternoon, Patricia," acknowledged Mr. Covington. He took a seat beside her with his newspaper. "Wish they would use some of that energy to get some chores done."

"Oh, Ralph…they're nine. Play is what they do. Look at how carefree they are. Life will present enough challenges for them."

From behind the pages of the London Times, he responded, "Yes, life is no picnic. We need to prepare them for it."

Dominic's entire family had been infected with Eeyore Syndrome…reminiscent of A.A. Milne's forlorn donkey friend of *Winnie the Pooh* books…gloom and doom cast on every event and most situations. Dom's mother had suffered the most

Finding Victoria

severely with it when post-partum depression visited their home just after Dom's birth. It never left. The tragic fallout brought divorce and a later residency in an institution. Ralph Covington never got over it. His son grew up in an environment where skepticism and caution were the norm, and it was all Dom knew until he met Bunny.

Dom was passive and introverted. Bunny, in contrast, had come from a household full of light and optimism. She was outgoing, direct, and confident. And despite their "oil and vinegar" outlooks, they were thick as thieves and loved each other as only friends can do.

As he grew into adulthood, Dom recast the pessimism as merely viewing the world as a realist. Bunny proudly proclaimed herself a full-fledged romantic; she believed anything was possible. It was a beautiful debate about life perspectives that always ended in a stalemate between them; however, the element of Bunny Magic always came up, which usually closed the argument in Bunny's favor.

Bunny challenged and told him that if he truly believed that, then he was a romantic after all.

She would say to him, "How can you believe in Bunny Magic yet call yourself a realist? It doesn't make sense. Dom, you are a romantic. Just admit it! Magic?"

"Well, you are an exception to reality," he would clarify, "because everything seems to work out for you. Or you believe it will." It always ended the same; Dom still believed Bunny Magic existed, but he still held fast to being a realist. And Bunny still always saw the glass half-full.

So, two weeks later, when the doctor gave her the diagnosis, at age fifty, even then, Bunny's first question for the doctor was an aggressive "How can this be treated? What do I have to do?" Meanwhile, her husband, Gordon, became emotionally immobilized and could not speak.

"It's called Multiple System Atrophy," the doctor calmly said, and then she paused, so the couple could process. "More commonly called MSA."

"It's like MS?" inquired a panicked Gordon, referring to multiple sclerosis. He was not making any eye contact with the doctor or his wife, but, instead, he was staring at the framed print of a Scottish castle on a serene lake, on the wall over the doctor's shoulder.

"Not exactly," Dr. Eckles shook her head. "It presents like Parkinson's in the early stages, which is why you noticed that slight tremor in your left hand." She was pointing toward Bunny. Gordon was listening, but he heard nothing. He did not want to hear anything.

Again, Bunny insisted, "So what is the prognosis, and what is the treatment? What's next? I'm ready," she said as she straightened in her chair.

"With proper attention and treatment, some people can manage the disease for quite a while, beyond the average…" The doctor was then interrupted by the patient.

"Be straight with me," Bunny insisted. There was a no-nonsense tone about her.

Dr. Eckles nodded in assent, "Okay, as I said, it's like Parkinson's…but on steroids. The progression can be very quick It will affect many body systems. The average lifespan is seven years after diagnosis, but you are already almost mid-stage. We can keep you on meds, and you can aggressively participate in physical therapy, which will help prolong the onset of some of the more debilitating effects."

Gordon maintained his blank stare. He thought of their three grown children who all lived outside of the country. Bunny could tell it was not registering for him. She was not even sure it was for her, but she continued to direct the conversation.

"Can you give me some guidance on what I should be doing, reading, researching? Are there trials that I can participate in?" Bunny was determined and hopeful.

Dr. Eckles handed her a folder with some information. "There's quite a bit in here that will answer many questions.

Finding Victoria

Take your time as you go through it. Call me with any questions. For now, we will continue on the carbidopa/levodopa. It will help with the shakes. Keep a diary of your symptoms and note any dramatic changes. Let's get you in here in a fortnight."

Bunny had been christened with MSA. She was forced to become a realist. Welcome to the school of Dom-think. The newly diagnosed and her husband thanked the doctor, left the office, and walked silently to the car. Bunny's thoughts were reverberating like the finale in a fireworks show. She told her mute husband that she would drive home and took the keys from him. One would think he had just had six pints with his forty-yard stare, almost comatose. He was badly shaken and in no condition to get behind the wheel. When they got home from the appointment, they decided to keep the news to themselves, at least for a little while. Even Dom was not told.

There are some partners in life who are the superhuman caregivers, who are willing to take on the world and more to provide for the one they love. And there are some who are more devastated themselves over the news to the point that they can barely function, but they perfunctorily carry out what they can in order to help their partner. Both types love very deeply and compassionately. Gordon fell into the latter category.

Dominic had no idea about the diagnosis until one month later. He was devastated by the prognosis and understanding of what was about to happen to his lifelong friend. Where was the Bunny Magic now, he thought? It had to be a mistake. His friend carried on with her usual optimism, but he became more astutely conscious of his tone and suppressed any Eeyore comments that might interfere with positivity therapy.

Eventually, Bunny had to quit her job at the library. It was getting difficult and tedious for her to perform any kind of keyboarding or written tasks. It was a small defeat.

The following month, Gordon suffered a massive heart attack. There was no warning. The doctors were perplexed as to the suddenness and the cause, but the family knew it was from

Finding Victoria

a broken heart. He died instantly. The children were not surprised. He had often prophetically told them in the wake of his wife's illness, "I can't live without your mother." And true to his words, he could not.

The children came home for their father's funeral, but they could not stay indefinitely. The youngest, Charlie, was the only one without a spouse or children and made accommodations to work remotely for a few months to look after his mother. But soon, he had to leave too.

It was Dominic, the pessimist, who then stepped up to support his friend. There was no question in his mind that this was what he was supposed to do. She had been his rock throughout their lives; it was time for him to be hers.

"I am going to leave my place and move in here with you," he told Bunny. Her two-bedroom cottage was small, but he knew he could make do. "I can continue to use my flat just for storage or for your children if they want to come into town for visits. We'll make it work."

"I won't have you do that,' she told him, even though the idea was comforting to her. She did not want to be alone…or worse, she did not want to be lonely; there is a difference. He didn't want that either.

"I have no family. You are my family," he told her, "And, I love you…unconditionally. I always have." It felt strange to say it out loud to her. They both had tears in their eyes. She nodded as she brought the tissue to her face, dabbing the liquid trails of salt water and mascara on her cheeks. Dom bent over her to embrace her. The silent hug that followed was powerful. They each wanted to be strong for the other. But then, as he went to stand up again, he wavered like an unsteady tightrope walker, and then he collapsed onto the bed, which caused them both to erupt in laughter. That, for a moment, made them forget about the MSA, Gordon's passing, and any other emotional nemesis. More tears ensued, but Dom said something extraordinarily comforting and out of character. "Tears are liquid prayers. Never

Finding Victoria

deny them."

In the weeks that followed, they spent many months laughing and recalling stories from their younger years. Playing cards and backgammon filled their evenings. Piping country-western music throughout the house was part of their routine, too. Dom never realized his dearest friend even enjoyed that genre. He had never even heard of Conway Twitty, but learned every word to the song "You've Never Been This Far Before," and they laughed uproariously when they sang the lyrics referring to "forbidden places."

Visitors came and went, leaving smiles and joy in their wake. At times, it was awkward, but Bunny often softened the conversations and asked how her friends were conducting their lives and what they might be looking forward to. She was the chief consoler and exhibited strength that seemed to know no bounds. Her childhood friend was in awe.

Dominic took Bunny to every medical appointment, carefully writing down any new information, so they could re-read it when they got home, careful not to miss a single suggestion, a minute detail. They never spoke of death, but Dom knew Bunny believed in God; she had been raised Catholic but had eased her efforts and intensity on the ritualistic and overt practices in attending church regularly. It was one evening, two years after the diagnosis, when Dominic realized the physical limitations had been settling in with great swiftness. The effectiveness of the medications was waning, just as they had been told would happen. Bunny no longer wanted to expend the effort to get in and out of the wheelchair anymore, and her permanent bed was set up in the sitting room. She knew at some point, her speech would be affected; however, presently it was strong, and she wanted more than ever to talk while she still could. She was never a woman of few words; her vocal chords were strong!

One Sunday evening, they were watching *The Antiques Roadshow*. It was set at Bowood Manor in Wiltshire, sparking another shared and eventual happy memory.

Finding Victoria

"Oh!" she cried, "Remember when we were there? God, that was so long ago. Gordon was out of town for work, and we drove up there with the three kids…two were still in nappies."

"Yes, of course, I remember," Dom bristled. "I lost your son, Charlie, in the crowds! There were so many vendors and tents everywhere. He just wandered off!" And what replayed back in his mind was the panic he felt as they ran from tent to tent looking for the small boy. Little Charlie had been lost on HIS watch, while Bunny looked after her two small daughters. How Bunny stayed so calm, he would never know. She was relentless and methodical, retracing steps and asking strangers if they had seen her son. All the while, she kept reassuring Dom that they would find him, when it should have been him providing her with the reassurances.

"He didn't go far anyhow," said Bunny, with ringing laughter. "Remember how we found him curled up in that dog bed with a Jack Russell terrier near the beer tent?"

"Bunny Magic strikes again!" chuckled Dom. "He could've been taken by a predator!"

"It's not magic, Dom. No such thing," she said with soft frustration. "There's only balance in life. The good and the not-so-good." She suddenly grew somber.

"You have to admit, with all the challenges you have been faced with, real 'magic' always seems to rescue you. Like a permanent guardian angel by your side."

In an atypically stern tone, Bunny said, "Let me tell you about this 'magic' you think I am blessed with…"

A confused expression emerged on Dom's face, and she continued with an increasing frustration in her voice that Dom had rarely, if ever, heard.

"Remember that day Sussex University sent those representatives to my house to announce I was the recipient of the Glendale Scholarship?"

Dom said, "Yes, didn't they take you and your parents to dinner? You wanted that scholarship so badly. And all the attention you got at school the next day…it was like you were royalty."

"Well, the day before the reps came, Amanda took me to a clinic to terminate a pregnancy."

"What?!" Dom gasped in surprise. "Your sister never said anything. Why didn't YOU say anything? Oh, God!" Dom's heartfelt emotion prompted him to grasp her hand tightly. "But who?"

She was silent at first.

"Remember that lad, Christopher?"

"The one you were tutoring in chemistry? Yes, I do recall him."

"Well, he forced himself on me," Bunny divulged and then added, "No Bunny Magic there. I think about that baby every day." Tears filled her eyes.

"Oh, God. I'm so sorry," he uttered in disbelief. Heavy silence pervaded. He regretted even mentioning the magic.

She continued, the anger in her building, "And did you know I had an older brother? When I was seven, he took his own life, and I was the first to find him and the rifle in my father's study. Is that magical, Dom?"

It seemed as if the pent-up anger over her illness was forcing its way to the surface like a geyser awakened.

Guilt-ridden, Bunny's friend got up from his chair, which was positioned next to the make-shift bed, and he embraced her tightly. She began to sob; the grief was overbearing. But the pain was coming from a place that was like finally letting the air out of a balloon. The pressure to keep everything to herself was relieved. Romantic no more.

"Oh, Bunny. Why didn't you share this before?"

"Because there are things in life that are sometimes beyond our control, Dom. We can't change them. Look where I am now…I didn't cause Gordon's heart attack. I didn't make myself get MSA. I can grieve, but I then need to move on. I can at least control how I react to these things. Right?"

Finding Victoria

"But you don't have to face things alone!"

"My faith has kept me in a place of acceptance; surely God has some plan in all of this, for me? I have to keep the faith. We all have goodness in our lives, not magic. But it's also counterbalanced with challenges. Some people call it baggage, and EVERYONE has it. Just because you don't see it, doesn't mean it's not there. But we have to keep moving forward with love and hope. I know when I get to the gates of heaven, there's going to be a sign there that says, 'Leave your baggage at the door.' You, too, must learn to do that, Dom. Pick your battles. Be free. Life is no place for self-created misery. Promise me you will let Eeyore go?" They both smiled at the Milne reference. He nodded in agreement. His emotions overwhelmed and stifled any audible response.

A moment.

The following months were not easy but were also filled with positivity and levity. Dom was the most loving and attentive caregiver Bunny could have had, even when she felt her dignity and voice had disappeared. They communicated through touches, but mostly through their eyes. There were no surprises and no miracles. Bunny Magic was never spoken of again.

She passed peacefully on her own terms. No morphine. No interference. Only a priest to give her the last rites, her children surrounding her, and her faithful friend. The air of pessimism had left Dom forever. The real magic, he realized, was in how his friend lived and faced her life. She was the strongest woman Dom had ever known.

And as the many mourners came to fill the church for the service, there was a very large sign propped up outside the door that read "Leave your baggage at the door."

Finding Victoria

6 In the Land of Beatrix

The August escape to serene Windermere's Lake District from London's frenetic life pulse seemed like a spectacular remedy for the exhaustion that had been infused into the lives of the Kelsall family. At least that was what Phillip and his wife, Clare, believed. The plan met with an intense volume of protest and grievance from their four children, who ranged from age eight to sixteen.

There was a chorus of "How long will we be there?" "What about my friends?" "It's going to be so boring!" and "What are we supposed to do that whole time?" The juvenile deluge became so overwhelming that later, Clare quietly urged Phillip, "Maybe we should take them somewhere else?" She hesitated to even say that, because he had been making the necessary arrangements for months.

The summer break from school always presented an annual challenge for the couple to resign themselves to — organizing activities that the entire family might enjoy together on holiday. This was certainly not the 1970s, when children found their own fun, and rarely did it involve parents. This duty mainly fell upon the Kelsall patriarch, and with it came the potential for either elated gratitude or severe criticism. Phil was the organizer, the overlord of calendars, schedules, and reservations. So, when he

Finding Victoria

heard what he took as a challenge to his sense of what was good for the family from Clare, his response was not unexpected.

"Everything is bought and paid for. We are going!" he firmly insisted. It was one of the few situations where his voice in household affairs could not be trumped by his imperious wife, who usually got her way, right or wrong.

"Well, I won't be blamed for the consequences," she absolved herself with a cautionary tone of "I told you so" and walked outside to the porch for a cigarette with a cup of tea in hand.

Tension in the house demanded the trip. Phillip's work schedule had amped up in recent months; he barely spent much time with the children, and even less time with Clare. The addition of a new chocolate labrador puppy, T-Bone, drew its own urgent attention.

"Someone walk the dog, please" became a daily afternoon request made by Clare, who worked from home, or from Phil in the evenings, from the kitchen table after everyone else had eaten and dismissed themselves. This was often followed by "I did it last time," punched back by sixteen-year-old Lucy, or then "I'll do it if someone goes with me," from twelve-year-old Cyril.

"I'll walk the damn dog!" said an exasperated Phillip to no one in particular, as he threw his napkin on the table.

The dog, thought Phil. He would have to go with them to the Lake District, making the five-plus-hour drive a little more interesting with this bouncy, furry creature.

The days leading up to the holiday only heightened the sniping and sarcasm among Phillip, Clare, and the children, driven by the promise of an unforgettable trip. The checklists were verbally recited each morning.

"Swimsuits, towels, sunscreen, pajamas…" Phillip's voice faded from the breakfast table as he multitasked, going outside to hang the laundry.

"We KNOW, Dad," snarked frustrated freckle-faced Annie, who was fourteen, but she only bravely said it when she knew

Finding Victoria

her father was safely out of earshot.

"Just do what he says," ordered Clare in her husband's support, even though she was just as aggravated as the children over what she felt was the constant nagging.

The real secret was that Mr. Kelsall himself began to second-guess whether this holiday was going to be such a good idea. He reviewed some of the activities he had planned. Clare was a lover of literature, so they would visit the house of Lake District poet William Wordsworth. They would spend a day at the national park hiking, enjoying the outdoors and the scenery. There were boat rides on the lake, fishing, and swimming. And the children would enjoy the trek to the house of Beatrix Potter of Peter Rabbit fame with expert gardeners to discuss the myriads of beautiful plants and trees, and lead visitors on their own planting experiment. There was even a tour of places in the show *All Creatures Great and Small.* The goal was to learn something new and to have fun. Plenty to do in his mind, he reassured himself. Good for fitness, education, and relaxation.

The old-fashioned alarm clock sounded extra harsh the morning of their departure.

"Turn that off!" moaned Clare, pulling the pillow tightly around her ears, as Phillip slammed his hand on the button. "Can't you use your phone with a nice ringtone instead. That sound is diabolical!"

"Defeats the purpose then," retorted Phillip as he sprang from the bed. He proceeded to the children's rooms, knocking loudly on their doors accompanied by "Wakey! Wakey!"

The frenzied click-clack of T-Bone's nails on the tile floor of the kitchen sounded like a hyper-caffeinated typist on the keys. The high-energy puppy was excited, oblivious to the long car journey ahead. The zombie children emerged from their tombs of slumber, and Clare made her way to the kitchen to make her usual strong black coffee.

"Bags in the driveway by 9 a.m.!" barked Phillip. He had his list out and was carefully researching the things to do.

Finding Victoria

    This was the prequel to episode one of "The Kelsalls Do Windermere 2024," and Clare already had uncertainty.

    Once the black Range Rover was loaded, everyone had peed, and the dog was put into his crate; Clare backed up out of the driveway. Phillip preferred to navigate to be sure they reached their destination on time. It was the one circumstance where Clare did not mind taking orders from her husband. Driving became a perfunctory task that didn't require much energy, thought, or interaction with others…she was gladly on autopilot.

    The careful balance of power among the children was disrupted exactly forty minutes into the drive when the youngest, Hugo, snatched the tablet from his nine-year-old sister, Jane.

    "Heeeeyyyy! It's still my turn!" screeched Jane, who made a grab back at the device, but Hugo managed to keep it out of reach, cradling it like a baby.

    "You got extra time," intervened Cyril; he had to stand up for the male family member. The gender advantage most often left him and his brother with the short end of the stick in family disputes.

    "Stay out of it, Cyril," Lucy snapped and punched him in the shoulder.

    This was followed by tongues being stuck out, one-finger salutes, pinches, and scowls. Clare emerged from her music and caffeine cloud, shouting, "Enough!"

    "But Cyril gave me the finger," tattled Annie.

    "We don't want to hear anymore," Phillip sternly said, turning to give his fatherly glare at the children. "T-Bone behaves better than you lot!"

    Hugo, with juvenile resentment, handed the tablet back to Jane. And within five minutes, they were friendly once again, sharing a computer game together, with the beeps and clicking noises emanating from it.

    Clare drove on with her co-pilot dictating. They stopped for a break about another hour later, when it was determined that the puppy had made a pungent mess in the crate. The petrol station

Finding Victoria

stop, called "The Chicken Coop," was somewhere off the M40, just short of Birmingham.

Jane and Hugo were holding their noses while vacating the car with exaggerated expressions of disgust. Lucy and Annie were in hysterics, and poor Cyril drew the short straw and had to help his father as part of the clean-up committee. Clare was frantically searching for her cigarettes.

The matriarch watched the family circus from a distance, puffing with urgency, making sure she was able to smoke the whole stick. Phil was pouring a jug of water on the floor of the plastic dog crate, and Cyril was minding the dog and disposing of the poo bag simultaneously.

"Girls…Hugo…go pee before we leave," directed Clare, who also needed to relieve herself after the jumbo-sized coffee. She stamped out the butt and followed the girls into a filthy restroom.

"Mummy, I can't go in there," Annie pointed to the almost overflowing bowl in the stall.

"They're all like that!" declared Lucy.

"Eeewwww…" whined Jane, supporting her sisters.

The four of them stood there in silence until Annie started sincerely gagging with her hand over her mouth

"Stop that! Come on," said Clare. "We'll drive to the next stop." They left the bathroom like a mother and her baby ducks in a single file.

Phil was putting the crate back in the car when Clare asked about another driving break, knowing what the reaction would be. He was already annoyed.

"We're not even halfway there yet," Phil reminded her, putting a very active T-Bone back into the hold. "You mean NONE of the toilets were usable?"

"We'll be quick at the next stop," his wife promised. She was already counting on another cigarette and a refill on coffee.

"Okay," Phil consented. "I haven't even gone yet. Let me at least fill the petrol tank here."

Finding Victoria

Everyone was safely tucked into the car while they waited for Phillip to pay for the fuel. It had been almost ten minutes.

"What are we waiting for?" asked Hugo, looking around, out the passenger window.

"Oh, no," sighed Annie. They all knew that Phillip could never just pay for anything without escaping a conversation.

"Lucy, go see where your father is," ordered Clare. That comment should have been put on a t-shirt for them all to wear, she thought. "Go see where your father is…" would sell millions. To be followed with the next installment of shirt in the series with "Wait, til your mother finds out…"

The tall teenager got out of the Rover and went inside the mini-store to find Phillip in a lively discussion with two older men with grizzled beards and hunting gear. They paused when she walked toward them.

"I know, I know," said Phillip to her, looking at his watch, following Lucy out to the car like a schoolboy caught playing hooky. "Very nice to have met you," he added over his shoulder, to his new friends.

The family was silently agitated when Phillip took his seat in the car. Socializing was his kryptonite for keeping schedules.

"Long line in there," he lied, and then looked at Lucy, who just rolled her eyes.

"For someone who is so hell-bent on schedules, you sure play a little loose with your own rules," Clare jabbed quietly to her husband, although everyone could hear it. Then she revved the engine and flipped the radio back on.

Looking again at his map, Phil returned to the captain's seat. "There's a place we can stop about seven miles ahead. We'll make it quick…I promise." Clare just kept driving without acknowledgement.

"There's the exit," Phil pointed out. "Get in that lane!"

"I know, I know," the driver returned. But, just then, a car quickly approached and cut in front of Clare. She jerked the wheel to avoid an accident. The whole family swayed in concert,

Finding Victoria

with shoulders bumping abruptly.

"My God, Clare! Pay attention!" scolded Phil.

"I got it. That idiot didn't have his signal on," she defended. The children knew better than to pile on.

When they arrived at the rest stop, it was eerily empty. Only one car was parked in the lot, a red Volkswagen convertible. There was no petrol station, just a small store called Wayson's for snacks and fizzy pops. Again, the mother and her baby ducks filed off to the restroom. Phil waited in the car with the boys.

"I'm hungry. Can we get something to eat, like crisps or something?" asked Cyril. He had turned his phone off now and had grown bored.

Hugo perked up in the far back with support. "Yes, crisps!" The puppy, too, joined in with whimpering.

Kelsall was not inclined to go into the store lest he incur the wrath of his wife. "Wait until your mother comes back."

Upon her return, Clare started to take out her purse, seeking a smoke, and then reconsidered. "Phil, you can drive now," and she made her way to the passenger side. She was met with Hugo's insistence on snacks, who started chanting, "Crisps! Crisps! Crisps!" Then Jane and Annie echoed in chorus.

Cyril volunteered, "I'll go get the snacks. Can I have the credit card?"

Phil turned and handed it to him. "Don't be long. We need to get back on schedule."

A few minutes later, the boy returned with several bags of Tyrrell's, tossed a few in the back to his siblings, and he handed the credit card back to his father.

Right then. Let's carry on," said Phillip, pulling back onto the highway with only the crackling sound of bags being ripped open and loud crunching. He instinctively reached for the buttons of the radio tuner in search of what would ultimately be a disastrous music choice, according to his family.

"Ahhhh, Duran, Duran…" He started enthusiastically and singing in terrible drunken karaoke style, "…and I'm hungry

Finding Victoria

like the wooooolf…"

There were protestations immediately with "Daaaaaad, no singing!" or "How about some music from THIS century?"

Clare punched the dashboard knobs, landing on something more contemporary to soothe the savage beasts. It worked. The next fifty miles were uneventful. There was even some snoring from the backseat.

"Slow down. Looks like the police have latched onto someone with a lead foot," Clare instructed her husband. She was watching the approaching police car in the sideview mirror, no siren, just the flashing lights of legal determination.

Phillip glanced to see the law pull up directly behind him. "That lead foot would be ME," he said with irritation. "I was barely over the limit."

"For God's sake," Clare threw at her husband like a dart gun, and straightened up in her seat as Phillip made his way to the side of the road with the police car. He fumbled through the glovebox for the registration; Clare was no help. Then he rolled down the window.

The female officer was not smiling. "Do you know why you are being stopped?" she asked.

"Apologies, officer. I was a few miles over," Phillip offered. The officer looked in the back seat and scratched her head.

"Those all your children?" she asked, eyeing them carefully.

"Most days I claim them," Phillip tried to ply a little humor to the situation. The children began to stir from their slumber and solitude.

"We had a call about a theft from a store a few miles back. Your plate and car description fit the details we have. Did you happen to stop at a place called Wayson's about an hour ago?"

Phillip looked at his wife for the answer. "Was it Wayson's?"

Clare leaned over, "Yes, officer. We stopped there."

Cyril was listening attentively.

"Someone walked out with several items without paying." The officer's stare met Cyril's wide eyes in the backseat.

Finding Victoria

"There's no problem here," said Clare, but when she looked behind her at Cyril, she became uncomfortable. He reeked of guilt.

"My son just ran in for some crisps…" Phillip trailed off. Clare poked his thigh, and then he, too, turned to Cyril.

"There was no one at the register," came the quick confession from the boy.

"Are you kidding, Cyril?" angrily commented his mother.

"Can I have your son step out of the car?" requested the officer.

Everyone began shifting in the back.

Cyril climbed over his siblings and stood outside the car. By that time, his mother jumped out and aligned herself beside him in protect-your-cub mode.

The officer was surprised at the youth's age. "Did you take anything else besides crisps, young man? Did you go into the register?"

"No, no!" Cyril adamantly denied. Phillip stepped closer, realizing the seriousness of the situation.

"Did you see anyone else in the store?" the officer asked. She took out a notepad, scrawling a few things down.

"Um, no…well, yes," started the terrified boy. "There was a lady with a big bag."

"What did she look like?" the officer asked.

Cyril gave the description, and his parents dialed down their anxiety, recognizing their son's minor role was of little concern to the enforcer of the law.

"Over five hundred pounds worth of cash and merchandise was stolen," said the officer. "I am doubtful this young man committed that crime. However…" and she studied him closely, taking a step toward him, "…you did steal and should pay for what you took, and I am giving you a warning for that. I appreciate the help on this case." She then turned to the distraught parents, "Can I ask that you come to the station to give an official report?"

Finding Victoria

Phillip was already fumbling for some cash in his wallet and handed a twenty-pound note to the officer to cover the cost of the merchandise. "For the crisps."

Clare emitted a sigh and then said, "Of course, officer. Where should we go?"

"Next exit. The station will be on your immediate left. You can follow me," the officer told her. And then to Cyril, she admonished, "You are very fortunate. The store clerk was tied up in the back room. That could have been you!"

She took down contact information from Phillip and held a finger up, indicating she needed a minute to call ahead to the station, then spoke to her partner, who was seated in the squad car. She waved the family to follow her as the trio took their seats in the car, but not before Clare lit up.

"What were you thinking, Cyril? You should've come out to let us know instead of just TAKING things without paying!" Clare scolded her son. A strong and steady stream of smoke was exhaled into the air with the sound effect of exasperation.

"Oooooh, Cyril is in trooooouuuble!" came a voice from the peanut gallery. It was Hugo's shrill voice.

"Shush, you!" Lucy loudly whispered, studying and trying to gauge the anger level of her parents.

"Everyone just be quiet," Phillip directed in a stressed tone, "We still have a way to go." And then in Cyril's defense, he added to no one in particular, "How the hell was he supposed to know there was a robbery in progress?"

The Kelsalls lumbered into the station. Cyril and Phillip were directed to a private room while the rest sat in a small waiting area. Jane dragged her doll to join them; it had seen better days.

"What do you need that old thing for? You're such a baby!" Lucy accused Jane.

Clare sat across from all of the children and just glared at her oldest daughter and telekinetically told her, "Don't start!" She looked at her watch. They were over an hour off their estimated time of arrival, which did not annoy her as much as it would her

Finding Victoria

husband, who had just resurfaced with their son beside him. Relief was painted across their faces.

"On our way then!" Phillip announced. Everyone stood on that cue and headed out toward the door. Back to the car.

"T-bone needs a walk, Phil," said Clare. But she felt some sympathy and volunteered, "I'll take him. Where's the lead?"

"It should be in the dog's bag," her husband relayed. A dog bag. They actually had such things.

"Hmmmm…not here," confirmed Clare, as she rummaged through the nearby bags and nooks and crannies of the car. Then the children began the half-hearted effort of looking around near themselves to assist in the search.

"I found a pound!" said an elated Hugo, holding the coin up proudly.

"Hey, that's MINE!" said Lucy, holding out her hand, "Give it!"

"Finders keepers," snickered Cyril.

"How about the lead?" Who had it last?" an irritated Phillip redirected.

"I bet we left it behind when you cleaned out the crate," suggested Clare.

"We can stop later and get another," said Phil. "Just keep an eye on him and make sure he does his business."

The day continued to get longer.

"Okay, T-Bone is all set," Clare affirmed and placed him gently back into the crate. He seemed content, and she scratched him playfully on the head.

Once they were on the road for some time, a voice piped up. "How much farther?" asked Lucy.

"Only about thirty-five miles more, thank God," responded Phil. "I would just like to sit quietly lakeside with a coffee and the summer breeze." He put the window down, and the fury of the wind barraged the seat behind him, waking Annie.

"Daddy, close the window!" screeched Annie.

Clare smiled and said, "There's your summer breeze!" to Phil.

Finding Victoria

Half an hour later, they were pulling up to the reception entrance to the resort.

"Wait here. I'll run in and get the keys. Be right out," Phil escaped the car with the eagerness of a child after such a harrowing day.

But when he returned, there was no spring in his step nor was there a key in his hand.

"Oh, no…" uttered Clare. "Now what?"

"They don't have our reservation."

"Will this day never end? What are we supposed to do? You set it all up ages ago," groused Clare.

"The manager said they double-booked the family suite. We have a voucher for a place down the road. Not as inclusive, a little bit smaller, but we don't have much choice."

Lucy, who had been listening attentively to her parents, chimed in with, "Does the new place have Wi-Fi?"

"Wait until we get there, Lucy," said an exasperated Clare.

The narrow country road took them to a row of quaint stone cottages with red doors and flower boxes. It was another hour before they would be ready for the family. Only two were available. More salt in the wound of an already long day. Decidedly, there would be no Wi-Fi.

By the time the two cottages were available, there had been arguments about which beds each of the children claimed, and the husband and wife realized they would be forced to take charge of each cottage separately, girls in one, boys in the other. No marital bed would be shared on this trip.

"Maybe we can sneak off to the lake in the middle of the night with a blanket?" joked Phil. Clare was not amused.

"Let's go get something to eat," said Clare.

"We'll go to that pub in town…I think it was The Angry Jester?"

"Appropriate," conceded Clare.

They entered, bedraggled and grubby, and the family took a table in the rear, where the only other inhabitants were a middle-aged couple, who sat sipping from a carafe of chardonnay.

The couple eyed the family with interest.

Jane loudly said, "Those people are looking at us!"

The four other heads of the children swiveled in the couple's direction.

"Leave those folks alone," Clare chided, and then looked toward the strangers and mouthed apologetically, "Sorry."

The woman laughed and smiled, "No problem. Lovely children." She then leaned toward her husband, Jack, and said, "That could've been us." The comment was made with a sad regretfulness; they were never able to have any children, although they had desperately wanted a large family. She watched them with interest. Jack nodded.

There was more of a quiet observance of the Kelsalls from their small, corner table. The family had taken up most of the oxygen in the room, but the couple did not mind.

The server spent at least ten minutes getting the family orders after several minds being changed and overlapping outbursts.

"I want what Lucy's having," whined Annie.

"You can share some mushy peas with Cyril."

"Can I get that on the side?"

"Is there chocolate milk?"

"What vegetarian options do you have?"

"I don't like the carrots."

"Two pints, PLEASE!" begged Clare.

"YES!" agreed Phil.

Clare looked over at the couple and apologized once again, "We're so sorry to disrupt your meal. It has been a long day for us. We drove up from London. On holiday. You know how children are."

"No problem at all," Jack smirked. "No children of our own, but we can see you have your hands full…in a good way. Nothing like family to help one get priorities straight." He was a bit reflective when he said it.

Finding Victoria

"You are truly blessed," added the woman. The carafe was almost empty. She offered the last of it to her husband. They shared an almost secret toast acknowledging the blessing of children and family. A joy they could never experience.

And in that moment, Clare looked at her family in all their raucous and exhausting pitch. She felt a sudden jolt of adoration for her annoyingly beautiful husband. The woman's comment and expression struck a chord.

Some time later, as the Kelsall family ordered puddings and coffees, the chardonnay sippers quietly slipped out the door hand-in-hand.

And when Phillip got the check for dinner, he turned to his wife.

"Oh, my God. That couple paid for our meal," said Phillip, shocked and confused at the kind gesture. "Why would they do such a thing?"

But Clare knew. She looked around the table at her chaotic but beautiful family, and she mouthed the words, "I love you," across the table to her husband.

Finding Victoria

7 Tit for Tat

"No. That painting is not worth the frame it sits in," stated Barnabas Worden, looking away with disinterest. He was a veteran dealer in antiques and anything vintage. "Have you any walking canes?"

"I still think you should reconsider a bid on the painting, Barney. It was done by a local artist who once claimed he had a nude Princess Margaret sit for him," said Garrick Lyons, the proprietor of Lyons & Sons Estate Sales in Ipswich.

"Bollocks, Garrick. You can't believe that rot. That story was never verified by anyone with a brain cell. No witnesses. It was all part of a campaign to prop up the artist's wretched reputation. His work is shit," Barney condemned. "Now, what about some canes? I'm looking for something exotic and expensive-looking." He removed his tweed wool cap, which meant he was preparing to get serious about some shrewd bargaining, like a boxer lifts his gloves to his opponent in the ring.

"I suppose you may be quite right on the painting," conceded the graying Lyons, but not giving in entirely just yet. "But it is a lovely piece for a sitting room, what with the peaceful swans and the shepherd…"

"I'll give you five quid. No more," Barney offered, as if he

Finding Victoria

were doing Lyons a favor. "Take it off your hands. I can likely get twenty for it. Fifty, if I can find some lunkhead who believes the Princess Margaret bollocks." Barney pulled a a wad of currency from his inner vest pocket and set a fiver on the counter. "Just leave the painting here until all of our business is done. I can't be long today."

Lyons pocketed the money, but he felt uncomfortable. He had known Barnabas for five decades; they had been childhood chums in this same town. Garrick knew what would be coming next…intense negotiations that always put him at a disadvantage to his old friend, despite easily shaving five quid from Barney's healthy roll of bills earlier for the painting.

"I've got a few canes in the back. Look over that lot in the corner that I just picked up from a manor in Somerset. Some unusual items, but I haven't had a chance to look through them all thoroughly." Lyons jerked aside a faded, dingy red curtain and disappeared behind it on the hunt for canes.

A very discerning eye, a poker face, and healthy confidence were the gifts of Barney Worden. He traveled the countryside scavenging farms, homes, and estates for diamonds in the rough. At sixty-eight, his stamina and strength still allowed him to haul tables and heavy tools among the many items he traded in. The vendors and dealers all recognized him by his signature orange Nike trainers and brown eyes. And he traded in everything: first edition books, elegant brooches, secondhand haberdashery, riding boots, artwork, and anything he felt he could unload at a profit. In a world with eBay and Facebook Marketplace, Barney was still the successful leg man for old school methods. And while some of his purchases did land on social media and bidding sites, he still made better use of in-person auction houses and trade fairs, which were the bread and butter of his career. He had even appeared on *Antiques Roadshow*, twice in England, and once in America. People across the English countryside knew his distinguished face and shrewd bargaining. And he could still get the better of Garrick, which was worth

Finding Victoria

something in his mind.

The clever peddler walked over to the corner where his old friend's recent acquisitions were piled up in crates and boxes. He quickly scanned for any outstanding finds before Lyons could examine them with any aptitude. Some fine china, silver-plated cutlery, old books in excellent condition, wicker baskets, and a collection of dolls with a dollhouse were among the store of potential treasures. He carefully opened one of the boxes to find some albums from the 1970s and held up a *Saturday Night Fever* soundtrack.

"THAT will not be for sale, my friend," said Garrick authoritatively, who emerged from the back room with four canes in his hand. "I found you a few walking sticks. One's in pretty obscene condition, but the other ones look respectable."

Turning quickly, Worden had a ready, not wholly honest, rebuttal on the album stakes. "This album's gone down in value. You'll get a much better return on Pink Floyd or a Simon and Garfunkel *Bridge Over Troubled Water*," and then changing topics, "Let me see what you have there." He was still clutching the disco album, diverting his friend's attention.

"This is hand-carved, but the rabbit head looks a bit demented," scrutinized Barney, examining the canes.

"Came from some dealer in Yorkshire. They're all a little demented up there," Garrick laughed.

"Somewhat crude and not as vintage as you might think. Hickory?" added Barney. "I'll take it."

Garrick nodded, and it was set aside.

"The others don't interest me."

"Let's take a closer look at those vinyls," said Garrick as he lifted the box, but knocked over a few items; one was an old hardshell piece of luggage with a crushed portion where the lock was once in working order. "Pick that suitcase up, would you, Worden?"

While Barney obliged his friend, an exclamatory cry of "By God! *It's Dark Side of the Moon*!" came from Garrick. He waved it

Finding Victoria

over his head like a marooned sailor wanting to be rescued.

Barney had planted the Pink Floyd on top of the pile as a decoy to divert attention from the prized *Saturday Night Fever*.

"Look at this disgusting old, tired thing," Barney pointed at the suitcase. "The lock is impossible to open." He had been tenaciously jiggering the mechanism without success.

Exasperated, he gave up and said, "I'll take this," pointing to the suitcase, the album, and the painting. You can have the Pink Floyd."

It had been the mint condition Travolta tunes he had been after all along. Skillful diversionary tactics. They worked almost every time with Garrick. *The Saturday Night Fever* album was undoubtedly worth more than the Floyd, with its scratched cover and missing record sleeve.

Garrick shrugged, "Not sure what you want with the suitcase, but okay." They bartered without too much arm-bending.

"I'll be back tomorrow to have a look at those books. I'm still searching for a first edition *Charlie and the Chocolate Factory* with a pristine dust jacket. I have an American buyer interested in it. Have a good evening." And he left with his loot.

Barney's modest cottage for one was only a few miles from the town proper and filled with the valuables and favorite collectibles of his thirty-five-year trade. The exquisite collection of canes was evident everywhere, some in metal receptacles, and others hanging in prominent places on the wall. Some oak, mahogany, and a few hand-carved shillelaghs he had managed to win in a card game long ago in Cork that ended with a fist-fight and a quick escape. The bookcases held an eclectic library of literary voices from political figures to children's authors.

There was little evidence of a feminine touch, but women had indeed frequented the place – often. However, in the recesses of the nooks and crannies of history and past lives that emanated from the furniture and other vintage bounty, one might find a contemporary half-full perfume bottle of Jo Malone Wild Bluebell, a pair of women's wellies in the shed, a dish towel

Finding Victoria

with flower patterns, or some exotic spices in the kitchen that Barney never used himself. Ladies loved Barney. He lavished attention and tokens upon them and even loved some of them.

His relationships were wildly passionate and fulfilling. But his wanderlust prevented him from establishing any permanent arrangements, usually leaving him or someone else with another scar on a passionate heart. A woman might move in for months or even a few years, but the traveling he needed to do for work sometimes left a paramour in the cottage for many days at a time, and there would be awful "Dear John" notes left behind when he returned home. He was not sure why he kept the few missives, but he did. He would re-read them from time to time, in his loneliness. They were safely tucked under the dusty Victorian mantle clock. He never minded being alone, but it was the loneliness that wore on him like waves on a shoreline.

He set the *Saturday Night Fever* album on the saddle seat of the Windsor chair in the corner, slid the painting behind several others he had put against the wall in the guest room, and poured himself a cognac before settling into the depths of a soft-cushioned puce-colored 1960s era sofa he had purchased from a very attractive dealer named Wendy in Glastonbury years earlier. He knew he had overpaid for it, but her smile and high cheekbones had won him over, and he had been in the black that day by several hundred pounds.

Taking his first sip, he looked at the suitcase in the hall that looked like it had been put through a trash compactor. He imbibed on another thoughtful taste of the cognac and indulged his curiosity over the suitcase; both prompted him to get up.

Rummaging through the tat drawer in the kitchen, Barney found a screwdriver among the rubber bands, pens, and other inconsequential clips, magnets, and keys with unknown locks. Jamming it in the seam on the side of the case, he finally propped it open. A cascade of envelopes spilled out onto the floor of the foyer. They were dingy and faded, but the ink was

Finding Victoria

strong and legible.

The disappointment was palpable, and Barney took a good final gulp to finish his drink. Nothing more than a pile of ancient letters. He really had hoped there would be something of viable value, like jewelry, fine clothing, or some other forgotten, unique collectible. His instincts had let him down this time, and he was not about to share this defeat with Garrick. Barney had already one-upped him with the album swindle.

And as he bent to collect the faded letters, he saw the elegant lilt of the penmanship, and, intrigued, Barney randomly picked up a handful and took them to the sofa, opening one. It was addressed to Gilbert Babbage, 7 Knollwood Grove, Minehead, Somerset. The postmark was the year 1900.

"You certainly are a long way from home," Barney said aloud when he saw the address. He poured himself another drink, settled into the sinking cushion of Wendy's sofa, and started reading.

30 January 1900
Dearest Gilbert,
I received your last letter with a heavy heart to learn of your mother's passing. She was always very kind to me, and I will cherish the beautiful silver locket she gave me so many years ago more than ever now. Oh, how I wish I could be there to comfort you in this very difficult time.
My sister, Blanche, has told me that your medical practice has been successful, with many complimentary reviews by people in town for your thoughtful manner. She said you were especially attentive to her young Frederick when he had bronchitis. Blanche said Frederick shows no signs of relapse.
I continue to teach piano lessons from home to earn some income. David can no longer work, but his illness has calmed in recent weeks. Praise God for that. I can work and care for him without too much trouble. Neighbors have been very kind, sending many baskets of goodies and meals for us, but it is my loneliness that desires a remedy. Perhaps that is divulging too much. I will pray for your mother's soul. God will care for her now. I look forward to

Finding Victoria

your next letter, my love.
Until then, I am your Sophia

Barney looked for a return address on the envelope: S. Waite of Brighton, and then picked up a second.

28 February 1899
My Dearest Gilbert,
Thank you for the heartfelt poem that arrived in your letter just one day after St. Valentine's Day. I wish I could place it under my pillow so that I may dream of you. David never remembered the day of love. I commissioned a painting of him by the Widow Fleming as my gift to him. It is coming along nicely.
I have heard from your brother that you and Sarah are expecting a child. What a blessing. I hope if it is a boy that he favor you with sparkling eyes. And if it is a girl that she possess your rich dark curls. God seems to have other plans for David and me. But I have faith there will be something good in store for us yet.
My nieces from Canada will be arriving next month for a visit. My brother has business in London, and the girls will be quite a help to me since two servants left over David's temperament.
Some days I feel as if my heart cannot bear the pain when I think of you, but then I cherish the words in your letters. And I have to accept what we have, as to have nothing at all would be unbearable at best.
Still, your Sophia

Barney picked up a third and fourth letter without pause. It was like eating a bag of crisps, where one is not enough. The dates changed, but the sentiments were always the same. The tortured soul of Sophia bled through the calligraphy. He arranged them in rows of chronological order based on the postmark. They began in 1887, and some were as late as 1941. He longed to know the contents of the letters written by Gilbert to Sophia, although it was not too difficult to determine based on what Sophia wrote. There were over one hundred letters in total, with some gaps in the timeline, some larger than others.

Finding Victoria

Barney read many of them late into the night, with a break for a microwaved entrée of processed meatloaf, when he realized it was almost 2 a.m. He began dozing off until he read the account of David's physical abuse of Sophia. It was jarring for a Victorian-era description.

"Good God!" Barney sighed. Although he had suspected this from the tenor of her relationship with her husband, this letter spelled it out with specifics. Barney had been drawn into this ghostly drama of the past, and he resigned himself to read more, but only after he got some sleep.

The following morning, it was Garrick's phone call that woke Barney up. His ringtone of Blondie's "Call Me" blasted from the dressing table.

"Sold that Pink Floyd for ninety pounds when I opened up this morning. First customer! You are not at the top of your game, my friend. You took that *Saturday Night Fever* instead. Bad choice," boasted Garrick. "What time are you coming by? It's nearly ten."

"Hmmmm. Wouldn't have paid that much for the Floyd, but I suppose things are only worth what the demand dictates," conceded Barney, knowing he could get even more for the Travolta lightning rod.

"Anything in that old suitcase?"

"Nothing of real value. Don't think I'll be stopping by today. I've too much to do yet. I may head down to London," lied Barney. He intended to remain at home to finish Sophia and Gilbert's story. He would not normally get so sucked into a vortex of sentimentality, but these letters intrigued him.

"Well, I am going to let Peterson and Gillingham go through the rest of that Somerset lot then."

"That's fine. Just keep your eye out for that Roald Dahl for me. Bye."

After a quick breakfast, Barney returned to his rows of Sophia's piecemealed life story. He wondered if Gilbert was as prolific as his Sophia?

Finding Victoria

There had been tragedies and triumphs, but always the same longing. It was clear that the letter writer and the receiver both deeply loved each other, and their marriages were not what they ought to be. There were references to their younger years, and there were hints that they were together once, before their marriages. While the final letter did disclose some details, the burning question of "Why weren't these two together?" echoed in Barney's mind. It was an obsession that, momentarily, surpassed his focus on his cross-country hunt for antiques.

22 August 1941
My Gilbert,
I received your recent letter dated 29 July. I worry every day for our young men in the war. In some ways, it makes me grateful I do not have a grandson going to fight. My neighbor, Mr. Brantford, believes the Americans may get more involved.
I have my health and am grateful to be able to volunteer in town with some of the causes for the war. Living alone does not offer much solace, but to do God's work with the church during such dire times does provide a sense that I am loved and needed.
Blanche told me of your automobile accident, and I pray that your broken leg continues to heal.
After all this time, I would very much like to see you, even though it has been a lifetime. I am no longer that same young woman you fell in love with at Brighton Beach. But perhaps I am a better version of her now. And though age has probably found you too, I will always still see my dark-haired Lancelot.
Forgive my forwardness, but perhaps we should have been together some time ago, but I suppose we cannot question God's plan.
We are both alone now. I understand if you do not wish to see me, but I am too old now to be cautious about life any longer. I have to live. I have to do the things in life I want to do. You were always part of my life plan.
I look forward to your response.
Deepest Love,
Sophia

Finding Victoria

As soon as he finished reading the final letter, Barney leapt to the desk and began pecking at the keyboard with the monitor humming at him. He did not step away from his computer for another two hours. He was obsessed.

He had been scouring genealogy sites and searching names and places. Gilbert Babbage! He had lived in Minehead until he died in 1960 at age ninety-two. No obituary, just a brief death notice. But when he searched the directory for 7 Knollwood Grove, another Babbage name turned up: Vanessa Babbage. A daughter? No phone listing.

And in an impulsive move, Barney decided he would take on the five-hour drive to Minehead and find out what exactly happened in his suitcase love story. He had to know. There would be antique opportunities along the way, he justified. Why not? He may even be able to sell the *Saturday Night Fever*.

The drive seemed to pass quickly. He did become nervous when he found he was within a ten-mile radius of Minehead. He turned off the A39 at Williton to make himself presentable and to purchase some flowers as a courtesy for Vanessa Babbage, whoever she was, or for anyone else who might help him.

He pulled into the long gravel driveway to a lovely cottage with a view of the Bristol Channel. The property was well-manicured with healthy red rose bushes, California lilacs on either side of the door, and an assortment of other perennials framing the vast property along the fencing. A woman in a straw hat was on her hands and knees pulling weeds from one of the flower beds on the side of the house. She promptly stood up at the sound of Barney's approaching car.

"Good afternoon!" she called to Barney, waving with her gloved hand. She wiped the perspiration from her forehead with the back of her forearm. "Can I help you?" Barney was pleasantly surprised to find a woman of his own age or perhaps younger. Flecks of graying streaks were blended in with brownish-blonde hair. Shadows of middle age tinged her slim figure. He was intrigued now more than ever.

Finding Victoria

"Yes, hello," he smiled. "I am looking for a Vanessa Babbage?"

The two were face-to-face.

"I am Vanessa Babbage."

"Oh, well, yes. You will think this quite strange, but I wondered if you might know of a Gilbert Babbage?" The white bouquet of roses hung in his left hand at his side.

"Did you bring those," she pointed at the flowers, "for Gilbert?"

They both smiled; tension was eased.

"Gilbert was my great-grandfather," she said.

"Mind if I ask you a bit about him?" shyly asked Barney. He was noticing the stray wisp of hair that had blown down into her face as she swatted it away. There was a simple country beauty about her. He was no longer the confident and domineering bargain hunter but a weak-kneed schoolboy. "These are for you, if you'll oblige me." He handed her the flowers.

"Thank you. Now, exactly who are you, and what is your interest in my great-gran?" She inhaled the flowers.

"Oh, right," Barney commented, "I have some personal and historical items that belonged to him. I'm Barney Worden; I'm an antiques dealer. I was trying to track down any relatives of Gilbert, and I suppose I found one!"

"Please come inside where it's cooler, and we can talk about Gilbert." Vanessa softly guided Barney by grabbing him by the arm, in an almost familiar way, and led him into the cottage.

In the entryway, Barney saw some beautifully adorned canes tucked and leaning in the corner. He had the nose of a bloodhound when it came to finding treasures of the past.

"Oh, those belonged to Gilbert," Vanessa informed him, noticing his attention on them. "I've been told they were gifts from a mysterious woman. There are some interesting family stories about great-gran. Please, let's go into the sitting room. I have to wash these hands first. Make yourself comfortable," she pointed to some chairs and disappeared around the corner.

Finding Victoria

Worden paused to admire the heads of the canes and knew they held value, but he was thinking more about the sentimental value for the man he had gotten to know quite intimately in only the last twenty-four hours. After examining the canes, he followed his hostess to the sitting room and sat in a cozy high-back chair.

The room was compatibly eclectic with his own style and taste, and there was much to view. There were antique paintings of fruits and such, alongside abstract art of the '60s. A shelf filled with colorful vintage perfume bottles and atomizers was hovering over an antique writing desk covered in vintage American *Sports Illustrated* magazines. In one of the corners was a large, half-dead bamboo plant almost reaching the ceiling; it had overgrown its pot, which was on the floor. Then his hostess entered the room, a little less disheveled, a little more interesting.

"Was not expecting guests, but this will have to do," Vanessa said, looking around the room. "Now, how would you like to proceed here? Would you like to ask questions, or shall I tell you what I know of Gilbert first?" She sat on a small powder blue floral-patterned ottoman and pulled it up close to where Barney was seated. There was a photo album tucked under her arm, and then she placed it on her lap so they could both view it. A scent of lavender and earth brushed over him when she sat down. Pleasing.

Vanessa provided the outline of a story that Barney already knew, with a few gaps filled in but with some vital details still missing. Before too long, an hour had passed.

"Forgive my manners. Can I get you some tea?" asked Vanessa, getting up from her perch.

"Well, yes, that would be lovely." And his eyes followed her from the room.

When she returned, she carried a vintage tray with the tea and a spread of cucumber sandwiches, cheese cubes, and biscuits.

"I wasn't quite sure if you might be hungry?" she offered.

"Oh, that's fine. Thank you," he graciously indulged himself,

Finding Victoria

reaching for a little of everything. He asked more about Gilbert.

"Now, did Gilbert and this woman ever reunite?"

"No one knows for sure," commented Barney's hostess. "My great-grandfather was quite a private person after he became a widower. We do know there was an unfamiliar older woman who attended Gilbert's funeral. She seemed exceptionally grief-stricken, and she was alone. My mother spoke to her, but I never knew what was said."

It was then that Barney told her of the letters. And he went out to the car to retrieve the suitcase. When Vanessa had finished skimming through them, she had tears in her eyes.

"Oh, my God. I recognize that suitcase too!," she looked at Barney. "There's a story here! Poor Sophia! How did that suitcase get out into the world? What of Gilbert's letters?"

"I'm not much of a romantic, but I agree about the story," he said. "Unattainable love is painful," and he thought of the letters on his mantle at home.

"Well, they had the love between them; it was the opportunity to be together that they lacked. Seems a waste."

Barney grew quiet.

"You know, there are some things of Gilbert's that I have never gone through before. I do wonder if there might be some more clues about Sophia?" pondered Vanessa.

"Now YOU are obsessed," Barney laughed.

"Would you like to stay for dinner, Mr. Worden?"

"Very much."

That afternoon, they were learning Gilbert and Sophia's story together. But more importantly, Barnabas Worden was writing the beginning of his own love story that began with the purchase of a beat-up old suitcase.

Finding Victoria

Finding Victoria

8 Lords, Lads, and Lairds

Somewhere within the concentric urban ripples radiating from the city center of London, there is a pub called The Sidetrack, aptly named because of its proximity to the train tracks that are a mere thirty feet from the back east quadrant of the building. It brings new meaning to *intestinal rumblings* or *shitting your pants* if you are in the loo when a train runs by.

The Track, as it is locally known, is a lively place most days and was the second home to many of the locals who had quite a metaphoric stock portfolio of regular cash investments in its lagers and ales. The manager, Paddy Lynch, had a broad, sterling pound smile when he locked up in the wee morning hours of each day. He knew another business day ensured his comfortable future retirement. He tipped his hat to the heavens each time he turned the key in the lock in homage to his Da, who took over the pub in 1952 from his grandfather. It was a ritual the red-haired owner performed at each daily closing, partly out of respect and partly out of superstition. He had been blessed with good fortune. No need to change habits now that might disrupt the balance of the universe, as his wife, Izzy, said.

And just when it seemed Paddy had left his establishment, he was returning as the sun's pre-dawn tentacles outstretched against the morning horizon. The jingling of Paddy's keys

Finding Victoria

could be heard attacking the lock. His ancient wooden door faced the intersection of the active street corner. It was something of a landmark for people in need of directions; no need for a map.

"Just look for the green sign with the railroad tracks above the door."

"Go two doors down from the Sidetrack pub, the one with the green wooden tables in front."

"Turn right at the corner of Sproule St. and Winston Road. You can't miss the sign in Gaelic-style lettering: The Sidetrack. Then go about 2 streets south."

Other businesses along the street were also awakening. The Sidterack was the linchpin in the neighborhood. They all looked after each other, but Paddy was tacitly elected the ringleader.

It was a normal tavern, but it had a secret garden area not far from the rumbling of the tracks. Sometimes, a small local band might play there on a makeshift stage, or private parties were thrown there, but the regularity of the trains running through was the main attraction. There was an excitement in it. The thundering room shook violently for maybe fifteen to twenty seconds. And in the back of everyone's mind was the thrill of wondering if the cars would remain on their tracks. The risk was small, but still, the danger was alluring. It was an attractive anomaly that no other pub in London had.

The lunch throng consisted of a healthy mix of tourists and local business folks grabbing a pint or a sandwich on a lunch break. But by late afternoon, as Billy Joel might say, "The regular crowd shuffles in..." The usual suspects were led by Rodney Fraser, a gregarious handyman of about fifty-ish, who made his own hours, which revolved around the pub's social agenda. His comfort and familiarity with The Sidetrack often elicited misdirected inquiries by customers who thought him to be the owner or manager in some capacity. The irony in it was that Rodney knew most of the answers. He carried a confidence about The Sidetrack that even Paddy didn't have.

Finding Victoria

"What's on tap today?" from a group of blatantly American tourists: men in their button-down shirts, probably chosen and packed by their wives or significant others.

Rodney rattled off in natural cadence, "Camden Hells, Sambrook's Wandle, Murphy's, Guinness…give Inch's Cider a taste."

"Can I get chips with that?" asks a customer.

"'Course, you can get chips with anything on the menu!" retorts the Scottsman.

"How old is this place?" asks another.

"This here establishment has been in the Lynch family since 1922. 'Afore that, it was run by a group of brewery owners from the Midlands who wanted to unload it after the economy tanked in the early '20s. Noble Lynch, a grand farmer, took a chance on it with his family's money after leaving Cork. It was a gamble, but the man had God and the luck of the Irish on his side!"

"Where's the loo?" a young woman inquires.

"Back corner," Rodney would point, but then add with a chuckle, knowing the next train was due, "It might rock your world, lass."

Rodney's tall stature and sturdy build gave him a presence at the bar. He looked like a bouncer, complete with tight white t-shirt, tattoos, work boots, and a sparkle in his blue eyes. A coveted signature gold signet ring on his left hand with the letter "F" stood apart from the rest of his attire. The receding gray hairline suited him, and he took no offense with anyone, though he seemed ready to pounce at a moment's notice for a scuffle or brawl if necessary.

Rodney was always the first to arrive at 3 p.m. and had a Camden Hells in his hand by 3:01 p.m. Paddy appreciated the business from Rodney, so the first drink was always on the house and sitting on the bar waiting for him.

Within an hour of Rodney's arrival, Algernon sauntered in. He waved at Rodney, who was a perpetual bachelor, flirting sincerely at the bar with any woman who entered. His sweet

Finding Victoria

nothings often landed him a catch. His current target was a forty-something woman in tight clothes and a buxom beckoning. Progress was being made. Algie, twice divorced, had to work a little harder for the attention of women. His tool was his friendly and honest approach.

"Ahhh, Rodney! Go figure the likes of you being here!" Algie teased his drinking pal, taking a stool at the bar. They had met at The Sidetrack one day ten years earlier. Both locals. They looked a bit like a Laurel and Hardy contrast side by side. Algie with the build of a tall pole-vaulter and Rodney with his intimidating "I can crush you in the back alley" physique, or as the latest addition to the WWE.

The waitress, Bev, tapped Algie on the shoulder. "Paul is outside with a round." She pointed to the row of wooden tables outside.

Algie turned to his friend at the bar to relay the message, but could see and hear that Rodney was knee-deep into his flattery mission. He decided to go outside to speak with Paul instead.

The handsome stockbroker, Paul Major, had only recently joined the group of regulars, but was welcomed into the fold for his sharp wit and adept insight into world politics, which he usually used to his advantage to instigate fiery and loud debate among the boys. When Algie approached the table, Paul was scrolling incessantly through his phone, surrounded by four pints on the table.

"Put that damned thing away," Algie squawked, and went over to shake hands as if he had not seen Major in years, when indeed it had only been a few days. Paul stood to greet him, and soon after, Rodney emerged from the bar with a grin and a pint of Camden Hells.

"And how'd we do?" asked Algie of Rodney, referring to his potential conquest attempt with the woman at the bar.

"I'm still working on it," winked Rodney. "Like a fine wine, these things take time, lad. I will be leaving with her, I'll wager." He took a seat at the bench beside Major but was still watching

Finding Victoria

the blonde at the bar through the window. "What's the market doing today, Paul?"

"You still thinking about your millions?" the stockbroker laughed.

Rodney held up his hand to emphasize the gold ring. "I'm telling you, sure as cows know when it will rain, that I am the laird of a Scottish castle somewhere. The family stories have been told. I need to hire someone to find the fortune that awaits me."

"You have been saying that for years!" dismissed Algie, taking a long draught from the pint.

Rodney stood up from the bench, "I'm telling you, it's true!"

And before things could escalate further, the philanderer of the group arrived, Anthony Masiello. He often escaped the madness of his family life in Balham to the corner retreat of the pub after a long day of sales. He outdressed even the barrister, Linley Covey, who made the occasional appearance among them. Masiello armed himself with arrogance like a soldier prepares for war. And it intensified with each drink. Bragging about his achievements was his specialty.

Oh, look…" said Algie, loud enough for Anthony to hear, "It's the resident overachiever!"

Anthony removed his Armani suit jacket, loosened his tie, and joined the others at the table. There were droplets of perspiration on his full, brown eyebrows. "This pint has my name on it!" He grabbed the extra glass and saluted with "Cheers."

"That one's on Paul," Rodney said to Anthony.

"I got the next one. Just made a major sale this morning, boys. Some American just bought a Bentley and paid cash!" started Masiello, his dark moustache twitched as he said it. He waited for a reaction.

"Okay, I'll bite," said Rodney, rubbing his hand over his thin-haired head, "How much did you make?"

"Obscene. These Americans…" Masiello shook his head, but

Finding Victoria

still teasing the financial highlight.

"Most of them are all show, living beyond their means," attested Paul skeptically, and he, too, loosened his tie, and finally removed it altogether.

"Paid cash?" rhetorically asked Algie, who was easily impressed but never felt outclassed. He had come from a humble lower-class background, somewhere near Bristol, and made his way to London as a laborer, mainly in construction. The gawky glasses slipped down his nose, and he was constantly adjusting them closer to his eyes. He, was without question, the most approachable and friendliest of the group.

Paul eyed Anthony from across the table, waiting for him to play his next line regarding the Bentley, but then made a strategic move of his own and changed the focus of the conversation completely. Outside of Linley Covey the barrister, the youthful wavy-haired Paul, at age thirty-nine, was actually the wealthiest among the group. Never married, but rarely without a woman in his life, the charming man had two cats and a flat near Victoria. His mother lived a short walk from The Sidetrack, so he often stopped for a few drinks at Lynch's place and then made his way eventually to his mother's for home-cooking. He was mainly the observer who threw comments in only when necessary, but he significantly impacted the discussion. Character analysis was his strength.

He was more interested in the complementary nature of this eclectic assemblage of accidental comrades. Their common thread: The Sidetrack.

"Rodney, I think your pudding at the bar is getting chatted up by that wanker with the Grateful Dead t-shirt," prompted Paul, smirking. Rodney was sufficiently distracted from the commission Anthony earned on the Bentley.

"Naaw," replied Rodney, "He's a plaything. Too young for her. She needs a real man. A Scottish laird to be exact," and he confidently patted his chest with both hands. "She's just passing the time. Patience, patience, boys."

Finding Victoria

Laughter abounded, but they all knew that Rodney would be leaving with the woman as promised. They had seen the miraculous nature of it hundreds of times. No one could understand his secret to success, and Rodney never shared it.

The late afternoon sun beat intensely overhead, and Anthony pulled out his Ray-Bans while everyone else was content to squint and carry on, not noticing. Paul made a mental note of it.

A slight man of about seventy appeared from the double oak doors with his worn blue jeans and long untucked button shirt. His shoulder-length, dulled, straight salt-and-pepper hair was a residual of the early 1970s. Teddy was the salt of the earth. A very quiet and gentle man who had a military background, but he had spent most of his life as a brick mason. He was a latecomer to the group but had been watching from afar in the early days when Rodney and Algie came in to raise a ruckus. No one knew too much about him, but he had his fair share of life challenges as an amputee. It was his companion, who garnered more attention, his pitbull, Tank, who sometimes came along with him.

"Teddy, old boy!" cried an elated Algie, who stood up and gave Teddy's good limb a high-five, his idiosyncratic move when the alcohol started to have its way with him. Algie was always a happy drunk with or without the alcohol.

Paul raised a circular motion with his hand for the waitress to bring another round. Newcomers were welcome. And just as Teddy took a seat, "the Lord" appeared.

Barrister Linley Covey did not indulge often with the boys, but it was a special event when he did show up at the Lynch establishment. A barrister by profession, Linley also maintained a lord title, but an inconspicuous one. He downplayed it. The Sidetrack crew respected that but couldn't resist the occasional jeering.

"Blasted tube repairs and closings!" Linley ejaculated with annoyance. When Algie approached for the high-five, the slap was returned with as much enthusiasm as that of the initiator.

Finding Victoria

Linley made his way around the table, shaking hands and clinking glasses with those he had not seen in weeks.

"Where the hell've you been, Lord?" asked Rodney, knowing full well that Covey had been the chief prosecutor on a sensationalized murder case that took place in Chigwell.

"Have you not read the papers, man? I've been trying to put a criminal away for life!" said the barrister.

"Of course!" teased Rodney. "Now that you got the conviction, do you think he really did it?"

Linley chose words carefully, even among friends. "The evidence certainly pointed to it. Anyone up for a whiskey?"

A few hands went up for the harder refreshments.

"Teddy, up for a whiskey?" The barrister made an effort to bring the reserved man into the conversation. Teddy seemed more than usually passive.

Anthony removed his Ray-Bans and challenged the Lord's dodge on the case question. "What about the witness who swears it wasn't just Roundtree who was there in the building that night?"

"Roundtree did it!" barked Algie. He was the first to pick up a shot of whiskey from the tray that arrived shortly after that.

"Arthur Roundtree was in the wrong place at the wrong time," suggested Anthony.

Linley looked agitated to be discussing work, and humored Anthony, but not before the strong voice of Rodney piped in.

"The man's prints were at the scene. He had motive, and he had no alibi."

Rodney's authoritative conclusion hardly satisfied the subject, but without necessitating more support from Linley, who had made his way to Teddy in the background of the debate. Rodney and Anthony carried on with their suppositions. Paul enjoyed his front row seat, cheering for Rodney all the way.

"What's happening, mate?" Linley compassionately inquired of Teddy in a quiet tone, away from the fray. Without hesitation and appreciative, Teddy said, "Tank was hit by a car this earlier

Finding Victoria

this morning."

Tank was Teddy's one true love of eight years. With everyone's focus on Linley's arrival, the absence of Tank was not addressed. The ferocious dog was the mascot of sorts for The Sidetrack. Paddy kept a special dish in the back for him; it even had his name on it.

Linley patted Teddy on the back, concerned, "What happened?"

"We had just left the park from the morning walk and got to the crosswalk, but a speeding car ran through the light. Tank tried to protect me, but he was hit. He needs surgery on both of his back legs. It's bad." The forlorn dog owner welled up. "Can't afford it. Need to decide in the next twenty-four hours. Doctors aren't even sure if he'll survive it." Teddy swallowed half of the pint in front of him. "He's with the vet."

The Lord was a lover of animals and had three dogs of his own, beloved terriers. He had seen Tank on several occasions at the pub as a protector of Teddy. They all seemed to have more balls with a few drinks in them and Tank in the vicinity. It would be a mistake to start a fight with any of The Sidetrack Boys under those circumstances. Odds were not very favorable for anyone who challenged them.

"Don't worry, Ted," assured Linley, and again, patted him on the shoulder, and disappeared into the pub.

Algie leaned over and asked, "Ted, where's our boy, Tank?"

"Out of commission today," said Teddy solemnly. This comment sailed over the head of Algie and was followed by a second annoying inquiry.

"Under the weather then?" asked Algie.

And then again, Algie commented, "He hasn't been 'round. We miss the old boy."

"Damnit, Algie! Stop asking questions!" growled a frustrated Teddy, who got up from the table and left.

Algie pushed the glasses again up toward his eyes, with confusion.

Finding Victoria

Paul tapped Algie on the shoulder. "What'd you say to him?"

Algie shrugged and scratched his head and then took another whiskey, nearly spilling it down the front of him as it made its way to his mouth.

Teddy was gone, but Linley reappeared with a large jar in his hand.

Paddy then stepped out into the rows of wooden benches and tables with a cowbell in hand, ringing it vigorously.

"Attention, attention! Our friend, Teddy, needs a bit of help. As some of you may know, our precious Tank was hit by a car yesterday with life-threatening injuries. He needs funds for the surgery, and he needs it fast! Empty your pockets with generosity for this cause. We're also donating a quid per pint to help out our four-legged friend, so drink up! We're open until 2 a.m. tonight!"

There were many surprised expressions among the customers, and the regulars reached into their wallets without hesitation. There were murmurs of "Who's Tank?" "He's a dog?" "I had no idea!" and "Poor Teddy!"

For the next few hours, it was like the final scene of *It's a Wonderful Life* when everyone in town donated to help out George Bailey. Coins clinked into the jar, and ordered rounds of shots and pints were plentiful, a spontaneous combustion of funds.

Paul watched and briefly respected Anthony who put a wad of cash into the jar. It grew into a competitive event among the tables. Business was bustling, and Paddy rang the cowbell every time a round was ordered. Tank was going to get his surgery. The cash continued to add up.

By 2:30 a.m., it was only Paddy, his staff, a few people at the bar, and the Rodney clan who remained past closing time.

Paddy went out to the front and said to Anthony, Linley, Algie, Paul, and Rodney, "You done a good thing here tonight. And you done it for someone you barely know, really."

"We're hardly strangers," corrected Algie.

Finding Victoria

And they all knew he was right. For years they had shared their grievances, their politics, their love lives, their joys, and so much more with each other over pints and chips, even though they never socialized beyond the confines of the pub.

"Okay, well, you boys best be on your way, so I can lock up. Thank you again," said Paddy. "I'll be sure Teddy gets this in the morning."

"Wait…Need to grab something," said Rodney as he jumped up to go inside the bar.

And when he came out, he had two women with him, one on each arm.

Finding Victoria

Finding Victoria

9 Life of the Party

Caroline Hartland shuffled into the kitchen, listening to the swooshing sound of her worn slippers on the cold ceramic tile of the kitchen floor.

"Coffee…coffee…must have coffee…" echoed in her head almost loud enough to be audible to the human ear. Then "Aspirin…aspirin…aspirin…" as she aggressively massaged the top of her throbbing head. Every strand of her blonde hair hurt.

She almost needed to shield her eyes from the threads of morning sunlight that were coming in through the edges of the closed curtains.

"Jodie, where's the coffee maker?" she asked the lively dachshund who hugged her feet. The canine merely paused at hearing her name and then continued to affectionately greet her owner.

"Okay, okay. Let me get you some breakfast first, then we'll talk caffeine," she said, grabbing the bowl from the floor and dumping a healthy amount of dog food into the dish. Jodie abandoned the love fest and focused on breaking the world speed record for eating a dog breakfast.

"Ah, here's my beauty!" Caroline announced pulling the appliance from the pantry. She wanted to kiss it. Realizing that she only had coffee beans, and not coffee grounds, was not good news, because it meant a very loud, painful noise would be required to grind the beans. She winced at the thought of it, but decided it was the hoop that had to be jumped through for any salvation from the hangover that plagued her.

The sacrifice was worth the effort when she tasted the first sip of liquid gold. She felt her brain knocking on her skull to get out. But within a few minutes, the aspirin and java were beginning the hard work of bringing Caroline back to the world of the living.

She was still standing at the counter with her cup in hand when she started thinking about things aside from her pulsating head. There were countless empty wine bottles lined up on the counter, and a half-full bin of crushed beer cans in the yellow recyclables container. Unrinsed dishes were stacked in the sink with two large pots still sitting on the stove. There was the residue of sticky pasta inside one of them, and hardening splashes of tomato sauce inside the other.

"Ugh, spaghetti…" Caroline remembered. She had invited some friends over the night before. It was an impromptu dinner party after her two brothers, Robert and Gavin, had dropped in unexpectedly from out of town. She had invited some childhood friends and their cousin, Malcolm.

She put the last two slices of bread into the toaster, hoping they would subdue the swell of nausea. But as she sat down at the table to butter the toast, the spread on the knife revealed chunks of some unknown origin on the knife that made it to the surface of her bread.

"What the hell?" she said aloud, and she took a closer look. It was glass! Glass in the butter dish and now on her breakfast!

"My last two pieces of bread," she lamented to herself, and then dumped them into the trash bin, followed by a huge scoop of softened, glass-encrusted butter.

"Coffee…" mumbled Robert, who emerged from the guest room. The twenty-eight-year-old was still in his clothes. He was the middle child between his bookend siblings, with two years of separation on either side. Caroline was the eldest.

Finding Victoria

"I smell it. Where is it?" Robert said, looking around, scratching his head, and opening his squinted eyes just enough to look for a mug.

"How did glass get in the butter?" demanded Caroline, ignoring his quest for coffee.

"What're you talking about?" he looked at Caroline with a confounded expression that changed quickly to elation when he spotted the target. "Aha, here's my beautiful lover," he said, pouring the coffee and smothering it with sugar and cream.

"I went to butter my toast, and there were shards of glass in the dish. Jeez, what happened here last night?"

"There WERE a couple of broken glasses…" He felt like a five-year-old with his hand in the cookie jar. No matter how old they were, Caroline always effectively played the older sister. "And there's some sauce on the ceiling," he added, pointing to a few sprays of red above them.

"Are you kidding, Bobby?" Caroline stood to get a closer look at the ceiling and swayed a bit from the suddenness of her action. Her head felt like it was ninety percent of her total body weight. "I barely remember going to bed last night," said the older sibling, pouring herself a second cup.

"The merlot was flowing…" recalled the younger. "And the rose d'anjou, and the pinot grigio. All in all, we drank the place dry, my dear sister."

"What time did everyone leave?"

"Leave?" Robert snickered. "No one left. They're all still here. No one was in any condition to drive. Gavin went to bed with Cara and Deborah. Stan and Malcolm are in the den on the floor, I suppose."

"What about Linda?"

Robert smirked with a glint in his eye.

"Oh, you didn't," said a flustered Caroline. The idea that her brother slept with her best friend irritated her.

"How could you? Really?"

"I am quite sure nothing happened there. Too much

alcohol," he blamed. "Besides, there was no other place for her unless she slept with you."

"Quite a house of lushes," laughed Caroline. "I'll need to put some kind of breakfast together for everyone. Coffee at the top of the list!"

"You missed most of the festivities anyhow. You went to bed early."

"Festivities?"

"YES! Glorious festivities!" attested Gavin, who made a theatrical entrance into the kitchen with a sweep of his arm.

"How are you so perky?" insisted Robert.

"Must have been the company I kept last night," alluding to the women who spent the night in his bed.

Caroline shook her head disapprovingly at both of her brothers. "Mum is right. This is why we are all still single!"

"I celebrate myself and sing myself!" Gavin proclaimed emphatically. "I think Walt Whitman said that."

"What does that mean?"

"It means marriage is for the insecure. I am comfortably single," Gavin poured himself the remaining coffee, which was not missed by Caroline.

"Make another pot," directed Caroline. "How'd you get that blossoming shiner?" She was studying his left eye. "Put some ice on it."

"Happily…" said Gavin, referring to the coffee, and then "What shiner?" His cheerfulness was annoying Robert.

"It looks like you have a black eye," she reiterated.

"No doubt one or both of the women wised up last night and gave you the what for," taunted Gavin's brother.

Gavin was looking in the hall mirror to get a closer look at his eye. And then seemed to have a eureka moment when he remembered the cause.

"You imbecile!" Gavin directed at his brother.

"That's when you hit me last night! I didn't think it would leave a mark!"

Finding Victoria

Robert was squeezing his jaw to conjure evidence of the punch he took from Gavin, which was the catalyst for the black eye. "Well, what do you expect when you deliver a blow for no good reason?"

"Oh, God, did you two fight last night? Over what?" asked the mother hen who was handing an ice pack to her damaged brother.

"No good reason?" Gavin mimicked his brother. "I hardly think accusing me of theft is no good reason. And it was done so publicly in front of friends. Hardly respectable. I didn't even get an apology."

"I only stated the truth. When father died, you helped yourself to his prized stamp collection and sold it for a tidy profit without consulting any of us!"

"Where in the hell are you getting that from?" pressed Gavin, who stepped closer to Robert and increased the decibel level.

"Oh, we all know how you eyed that collection from the time we were children. As I recall, you especially liked the ones that had birds on them. Remember when you took the American stamps with the eagles and shields on them to school? What were you like eight then?" Robert shared.

Caroline was giggling. "I thought father would have a coronary on the spot when he found out!"

"Well, I would've gotten away with it had you two not squealed on me," said Gavin. "Have we got anything to eat around here?" He peered into the cabinets.

"No bread, but I can fry up some eggs," offered Caroline, And then added another jab with "It was pretty low, Gavin, to to pawn father's stamps."

"I'm telling you both here and now, I did no such thing. You would both make shit prosecutors. There's no evidence whatsoever of what you are accusing me," he pounded a fist on the table for effect.

Caroline and Robert exchanged a familiar look of skepticism over their brother's non-admission. There is

Finding Victoria

the rub in dealing with a trio; someone always gets bullied and ganged up on. The tension escalated just as it had the previous evening. Robert stood up from the table and spouted a few expletives in a loud tone. Gavin had a mad look about him, and Caroline stepped between the two, hoping it was enough to prompt them to back down from each other.

"Ahhh, picking up where we left off, I see," uttered a drowsy and hungover, cousin Malcolm, who entered the kitchen. "Coffee?"

Caroline pointed to the counter from her defensive stance between her brothers. "Now we have an objective perspective on all of this. What happened last night, Malcolm…that you can recall?"

"Coffee first," he responded, and he poured himself a cup.

Gavin continued the argument. "I can't even remember the last time I saw those damned stamps! You two have probably seen them more recently than I have!"

"When do YOU last recall seeing them?" Caroline turned to Robert.

"No idea," quickly snapped Robert, "I suppose some time around cleaning the house out when we moved father to the nursing home."

"There! Exactly! I was not around to clean out the house," said Gavin with a prideful tone, convinced he was about to win the argument.

"STAMPS? Is that what this crap is over?" asked Malcom.

"Yes," hissed Caroline, "You were there last night. What the hell did you think this was over? Malcolm looked a little sheepish and reluctantly met Caroline's hard stare.

"Your father gave ME the stamp collection," confessed the cousin.

In unison, the siblings all cried, "What?!"

"I thought you all knew. He told me he thought I appreciated them as much as he did. Sold them all a few years ago," said Malcolm, who was now subdued.

Finding Victoria

Gavin's smug expression was begging for an apology. Robert was not yet prepared to eat humble pie. He hated it when his brother was right. Caroline was just relieved it was resolved.

"Just apologize," Caroline prodded Robert.

Reluctantly, he offered his hand to Gavin, who said, "Appreciated," and extended his hand as well. They shook.

Just then, a groggy Stan entered the company of the kitchen and looked at Gavin and Robert. "Well, lookee here…the life of the party! Where's the…"

"Coffee's on the counter, Stan," pointed Caroline, and she handed him two aspirin.

"Helluva party," mumbled Stan.

"So, I've heard," said Caroline, and she smiled at her brothers, who were reunited…for the moment.

Finding Victoria

Finding Victoria

10 The Margaret Matrix

My mother's favorite quote was, "You cannot make an omelet without breaking some balls." She cited it regularly, sometimes for effect and sometimes because she meant it. I just know that every time she said it, I laughed. Margaret Thatcher supposedly said it, and she certainly whipped up quite a few omelets in her time. So did my mother, for that matter.

I loved Margarets, and they seemed to haunt me most of my life.

The first girl I kissed was a Margaret. She had blue eyes and curly auburn hair clipped with silver barrettes, one on either side. I was twelve and she was nine. Sounds almost predatory and inappropriate, but this was when twelve-year-old boys might be more concerned with kicking a football around, riding their bikes in the woods, or catching fireflies with a jar on a sultry June night than thinking about girls. Some still thought girls had cooties. But I didn't. I was noticing the curves of Ron Benson's older sister, Bonnie, who was fifteen. The boys and I had the urge to salute her when she passed by us, but instead, we just held our breath. I suppose in a silent, covert way, we were saluting. However, she took little notice of us. And we were just satisfied to get a smile or a wave out of her once in a while.

My first kiss was mainly the cause and effect of a juvenile note. You know the one, "Do you like me? Check 'Yes' or

Finding Victoria

'No' sort of thing. Only this scenario was a little more sophisticated. Margaret was part of a trio comprised of Margaret, Lydia, and Gloria; the latter two girls were eleven years old, a full two years older than Margaret. And to be frank, Lydia was the prettiest among them with long, blonde, shimmering summery hair and the early suggestions of womanhood. Gloria took a distant third with her rugby stature but had a beautiful laugh to match her sense of joyful humor.

That summer, they had become something of a fan club dedicated to me. When I was just running around with my mates, those three girls would show up regularly. Statistically, it was beyond the realm of coincidental appearances. Sometimes they were just in the distance, acting aloof and uninterested, and then sometimes they would approach. One time, when I was wrestling with some of the boys in the July heat, they brought me lemonade. Just me.

Then the folded note came: "To Cameron."

It showed up at my doorstep accompanied by three brave knocks. My brother, Jack, who was fourteen, answered the door.

"Caaaaammm! Looks like you've got some admirers!" he teased so loudly, the whole family heard it.

I knew exactly who was on the other side of that door. Part of me was terrified, but I needed to behave as if all was in order, and that I had firm control of the situation in front of my brother, who was making obnoxious snogging sounds. I quickly hand-combed my hair.

I mustered, "Hello," but that was all. Cool on the outside, shaking like a leaf on the inside.

Gloria towered over her friends; her height conferred on her a natural leadership role. She held the note out to me and announced, "We need you to read this." Margaret stood shyly behind Lydia. My eyes paused a little longer on Lydia, but she outlasted my stare, blinking her naturally long eyelashes as I glanced quickly at Margaret and then down at my feet.

Unfolding the note, I noticed several points made in different handwriting, but the initial request was written across the paper in large letters: "Choose one," with checkboxes next to each of their names. Then beneath it, Lydia wrote," I think you are cute," Gloria stated, "I like your smile," and Margaret shared, "I love the way you make me laugh."

Maybe it was the word "love" that jumped off the paper, or perhaps it was the only comment that spoke to who I was, but I chose, and it was Margaret. This did not go over so well with the older girls, who never imagined that Margaret had a chance because she was younger. Age reigns supreme in the land of children. No adult wants to claim that title.

The romance was over within twenty-four hours. In a game of Spin-the-Bottle in a tree fort in the woods, I had my first kiss from Margaret, the girl who won me over with her words. We broke up the next day. I still have that note.

Another Margaret meandered her way into my life a few years after the note. Only she was called Maggie. By then, I started to resemble a young man; the boyish round cheeks had all but vanished, and my voice sounded more like a bullfrog than a canary. My blondish hair now took on a golden sun-kissed hue, with it falling into my eyes on occasion, which girls seemed to like.

The most striking feature of Maggie was her ability to put people at ease. You would swear that you had known her for a hundred years the first time you met her. I was introduced to her by my parents at a garden social. She was confident, yet not overbearing.

When she and I had some time alone that first afternoon, we walked along a shallow creek at the edge of the garden.

"You'd rather be elsewhere?" she smiled, "I, as well."

Her shoulder freckles were just subtle enough to notice in her sundress, but there was so much more of her to look at. I suddenly became self-conscious in my green collared shirt with brand name insignia next to my heart.

"Mmmm....I was not so interested in coming here at first,

Finding Victoria

but it seems fine now," I said, hoping she read between the lines. She did.

We whittered on in the garden for an hour before we realized how much time had passed. Butterflies and dragonflies did their ballet all around us as I gave her my story, not quite recalling exactly what was said. I know she was curious…about me. Her questions were like the notes of a beautiful melody, all linked together without pause, not intrusive, and I wanted the song to play on. There was nothing awkward about her. Her parents called to her for introductions to other guests, and I watched her stride up the hill toward the house with the pleats of her pink skirt kissing the back of her legs. We lasted seven months, twenty-two days. She broke my heart. I still have a scar.

When I headed off to university, I was still a virgin. So was Peggy Ashbury, the next Margaret. Scholarly studies were never my forte; I would rather doodle intently through my notes while in the lecture hall, sometimes making caricatures of my professors. I am told they were quite good. By the end of the term, I had a magnificent portfolio of drawings with entertaining spotlights on people who bored me to tears.

Peggy was ordinary-looking, with sandy brown hair and an average figure. I liked her somewhat affectionate nature but no-nonsense manner. When she said we needed to study, we studied. But that did not mean her foot would not slide over to me under the table in the library and stroke my leg from time to time as she looked at me demurely. When she planned an itinerary, we adhered to it, but that did not mean there were no surprises in our relationship. She tutored me in calculus and practically performed CPR to get me through World History.

When we finally did become intimate with each other, she took charge like a professional. I floundered through it, but I seemed to make her happy. I still am not certain she was the virgin she claimed to be; I found no evidence of it, and she could not convince me. And when I say she was no-nonsense, that is exactly what it meant…in everything…no pillow talk, no sweet-

Finding Victoria

nothings. That was fine with me…at first. But then I craved something more than just friends with benefits. Peg seemed content with the status quo. We lingered in that haze for another term. I needed more, and she didn't really seem to know me. Not really. Then I had to end it. Shortly after that, I flunked out of school. Another Margaret bit the dust.

I moved back home with my tail between my legs and my father on my ass. My mother was still making omelets.

"You'll work for me in the stables," my father resolutely proposed. We had an animal farm that would make George Orwell proud. It had an assortment of responsibilities, enough for anyone who wanted to pitch in.

It was 1985, the year of *Back to the Future* and Live Aid in London, and times were relatively quiet, other than Maggie Thatcher cracking more eggs on the world stage. I was in my early twenties, shoveling horse manure and training horses and dogs. Admittedly, being outdoors was an infusion of life for me. Nature provided all I needed as sustenance for my wayward soul. The smell of hay, sweat, and the sweet scents emanating from wildflowers and grass in the fields was enough. Business was prosperous for my family; my father even gave the occasional compliment for my dexterity with the dogs, both in training and grooming them. I thought I had found my calling.

There was no human Margaret in my life that year; however, I helped train a horse called Mighty Magdalene, which placed admirably in the Royal Ascot. And then there was my father's obsession with the Ray Stevens song "It's Me Again, Margaret" about a dirty old man who makes anonymous, obscene phone calls to a woman named Margaret. My father would begin to play the record always after his second whiskey and water when the workday ended, and then by the third drink, he would pour my mother a drink, grab her by the waist, and whirl her around the sitting room, singing to her like an old fool. In those moments, I had never seen my parents more in love, more joyful, and more euphorically drunk.

Finding Victoria

My parents sold the farm and moved off to Scotland somewhere between Stirling Castle and Loch Lomond; the land of William Wallace and "freedom," to live out their years together with Ray Stevens. As much as I loved being on the farm, I was eventually pushed out of the nest again, and with twenty pounds in my pocket, I went off to London like a true vagabond to seek my fortune and next lay. Those are the priorities when one is twenty-something. At sixty-something, seeking a fortune is for fools, and a lay is good fortune.

I was able to get a bedsit above a map shop in northern London, not too far from Cockfoster's Tube Station. After I took out my checkbook for my monthly rent and security deposit, I jammed my right hand into my back pants pocket and realized the only cash I had was pinched. It no doubt happened on the Tube. My expression of aggravation caught the attention of the landlady.

"What's the problem, love? Need a pen?" she asked. She seemed too young to be a landlord. She produced a fine-point Montblanc pen from her fine leather purse with her soft hand and finely manicured fingernails.

She was a step ahead of me; I was still stewing over my pocket being picked.

"Uh, yes, ma'am. Thank you. To whom do I make the check?"

"Margie. Margie Redmond."

Of course, I thought. Another Margaret. I smirked.

Two days later, Margie recommended me to a nearby carpenter who needed an assistant. What did I know of woodworking?

His large carpentry shop was partially hidden at the end of the road, but I could see the "Hiring" sign in large red letters, confirming I had arrived at my destination; the address was 168 Margaret Road. By this time in my life, the name Margaret may as well have been my own!

Here I was again, a jack of all trades, master of none. But

Finding Victoria

within six weeks, I had developed many skills and was a capable builder of butler's tables. My employer was a timid man who preferred to be called by his surname first and then his God-given name, which ultimately meant Joseph Little became "Little Joe". I observed his patience when working with the wood, his hands and fingers hardened, bashed, but strong.

"Now, look here, Cam, you have to keep sanding it here in the direction of the grain," he guided me, and then blew some of the dust from the wood piece. I nodded. The end result of his fine touch was amazingly beautiful.

Making butler's tables expanded to other nesting tables and bookcases. Little Joe was generous with his time for me both in the shop and out. We often stopped off at the nearby pub, The Smoking Dog, for a pint or two after the workday ended. I had nothing and no one to rush off home to at that time.

Conversations usually focused on politics or the idiosyncrasies of our upbringings, and although he had a couple of decades on me, there was something more fraternal than paternal about him, which I enjoyed as an only child.

I learned some months later Little Joe had a very beautiful daughter. Her name was…*wait for it*…Silvia. Not Margaret. It was probably a sign I should have paid heed to.

Sometimes life moves more quickly than you expect, so less than a year later, I married Silvia, with Little Joe as the best man. And just as quickly, within five years, Silvia and I divorced. But we remained friends, and I continued to work with Little Joe. We were partners in the business, and life was still good. My mother told me the marriage did not work because Silvia was not a Margaret. Part of me believed that to be true.

"The Margaret Matrix is real, son," she would say, and wink, "You are caught in its web."

It was one of the last things my mother discussed with me before she passed. I had forgotten about it until the funeral, when a small line of mourners approached me with their condolences. A woman in a stylish, dark-veiled hat addressed

Finding Victoria

me outside the church.

"Terribly sorry for your loss. You probably don't remember me, but I wanted to pay my respects," she expressed in a sincere and soft voice.

And I took a long look at her. No silver hair clips, but the same auburn curls framed her face.

We both smiled.

Finding Victoria

11 The Girls' Club

Raising a daughter is like a round of golf on an unfamiliar course. The game has the potential to go so many ways, and no matter how hard you try, things won't always go as planned. Edward Chambres let golf guide his parenting. Aside from the expected apprehension of being unacclimated for what is ahead, there are sand traps (dangers) you need to dodge, uncontrollable influences like weather (peer pressure), different clubs to figure out to use (parenting approaches), and no matter how hard you try, you need to accept that sometimes there are just bad days. The biggest misconception is that you believe you will be done when you hit the 18th hole! That's when a drink at the clubhouse may be necessary.

Edward was a life player, teased by the other players as the man of the triple bogey: three daughters. And he had raised them alone. Because he was passionate about the game of golf, everything he decided and did as a father was viewed through the lens of the ancient stick and ball sport. It was what he knew. Instead of reading books and articles about parenting, he paged through golf magazines offering some advice that he could apply to fatherhood, which required focus, patience, and some luck. For the most part, it was effective and had served him well. Addressing the ball was code for "Think before you speak."

Finding Victoria

"Follow through on the swing" was a direction to "Mean what you say." And then there's "Try not to strangle the club"…that one is a little more obvious.

Mr. Chambres carried on with an air of trepidation, but a strong sense of love and commitment to bringing up his daughters. He knew very little about girls. Raised in a traditional family, he had a mother who kept her thoughts to herself, maintained the household, cooked the meals, did the laundry, and looked after the children: four sons, no daughters. What did he know of women?

But when he was nineteen, he scored an ace when he met Sarah Nichols. Her curly dark brown hair was neatly pulled back, and her subtle dimples spoke to him. They had been queued up at the local post office in Yorkshire with a man standing between them, and Sarah at the front with a handful of documents. She was trying to sort and arrange them in some order, but one slipped out of her hands and floated behind her toward Edward.

If this had been a romantic-comedy, Edward would have gracefully caught the paper in mid-air, Sarah would have turned, their eyes would have met, and the rest would be history. But that was not what occurred. Instead, the paper swooped backward, even past Edward, and as he tried to grab it, he contorted his body enough to lose his balance. He captured the paper, but he painfully turned his ankle in the process of hitting the ground.

There were a few exclamations of "Oh!" and "Are you okay?" and Sarah approached him with "I'm so sorry."

Picking himself up, he handed her the paper. "I'm quite fine," he lied, feeling the throbbing in his foot and the embarrassment that landed squarely on him.

"Next!" cried the postmaster behind the counter, who looked sternly at Sarah.

In a flustered state, she cast an expression of further compassion toward Edward and stepped up to the counter with her papers.

Finding Victoria

Chambres was completely smitten. And when she waited for him after his turn in the queue, he felt nervous and blushed.

"Can I buy you a tea or lunch? I can't believe that happened! she said. She was more embarrassed than he was.

Edward took a hard look at her. She was quite athletic-looking with long, attractive, almost boyish legs streaming from the dark blue shorts.

"I have a tee time at two, but can treat you at least now," she added.

"Yes, sure. Of course," Edward cheerfully agreed, "But you don't need to."

"Let's go over to The Red Lion for a tea or something."

Crossing the road, Edward tried to disguise his hobble as best he could. His ankle was throbbing.

"Are you a golfer?" asked Edward as he pulled the chair out for his companion.

"Yes, I'm just learning. My father is quite keen on it and is teaching me. Do you play?"

"Oh, no. Not at all," he vigorously shook his head. He ordered a cream tea and cucumber sandwiches for both of them.

"You should join us sometime," she invited. "It would be nice to have someone else along, so I don't look so ridiculous swinging at the air." She was so comfortable with her dark-haired, raven-eyed companion. He had a warm and attentive manner. At one point, she had a brief moment of déjà vu when he reached for a sugar packet. And then it happened once again when he ordered a pudding just to spend more time with her.

While golf dominated the conversation, they discovered a natural rapport that resulted in an agreement to meet again. Sarah was on holiday for the month with her father, who was also conducting business, and they were staying at an inn nearby.

This was the beginning of Edward's love of golf and Sarah. The feel of the club and the ease he felt in her presence. Neither left his mind…ever.

Finding Victoria

The month passed in an emotional snowball for both of them. Then the young lovers had to say goodbye. Sarah gave him a golf club: a driver…long, sleek, with a metallic blue shaft. They each promised to write. A few letters had been exchanged for almost a year, but then nothing. Life had moved on for them…without each other. But Edward thought of her.

Evelyn came into Edward's life shortly after. He married her when he was twenty-one and newly christened as "quite a catch." They had a short romance, and Evelyn's fast, impulsive nature was on full display when she proposed to him in a moment of passion, and he, caught up in his emotions, impulsively said "Yes." And before any reconsideration could occur, Evelyn began spreading the news that they were engaged. Edward was more of a caddy in their relationship, but they were inseparable in the early years. Sarah was a ghost, but he had not forgotten her.

Evelyn was exciting to him; however, later he would describe her as a beautiful blonde bombshell, but reckless and rash. Evelyn self-declared herself a free spirit, adventurous, and immersed in life. There was some truth in the intersection of both of their perceptions. The couple was blessed with three daughters soon after their marriage.

In 1998, Mrs. Evelyn Chambres decided she had had enough of marriage, and she took up with a much older business mogul when the girls were three, five, and seven. This is not to say she did not love her children, but she admittedly could not handle the responsibility. There were the regular birthday and holiday cards sent to the house with gilded, embossed envelopes and fancy calligraphy, and the occasional phone call or text message. But the tenor of the relationship was one of acquaintances, and Edward's daughters felt a minor attachment to their mother over the years, but one that included a token financial contribution from time to time. Edward was the center of the girls' parental world, and despite the divorce, he considered his life to be a fortunate mulligan.

Finding Victoria

Some men find their best thinking is done in the garden, the shower, or the bathroom, but Edward's most satisfying reflections were done on the golf course. The girls had decorated his driver club (the same one from Sarah) with pink and yellow butterfly stickers and painted ladybugs on the shaft as a Father's Day gift one year. It always prompted mocking, and even a little envy, from his partners while out on the course, but Edward kept the club as it was, although it certainly violated the unwritten rules of etiquette decorum. He believed it to be lucky.

"What the hell is that?" a newcomer to his usual foursome observed on an outing to the course. Edward had stepped up to the tee with his adorned driver.

Chambres laughed, and another player, Calvin, responded, "Edward has a girls' club at home who look after him. It's his lucky driver, so don't mock the magic."

"Daughters?" chuckled the newbie.

"Triple bogey," whispered Calvin, watching the ball rocket off the tee and into the stratosphere. Edward turned and winked at his comrades.

Chambres' modest home in rural Cheddar of the West Country was less than ten minutes from the Isle of Wedmore Golf Club where he knew every groundskeeper, attendant, and caddy by their first name. His very own slice of heaven, or rather, slice of Cheddar he liked to joke.

On his days off from work, the father of three would have a coffee with Aly, the congenial woman working behind the clubhouse counter. She was about his age with strong arms and an even stronger personality. She commanded attention without much effort, and although she was remarkably plain, it was her optimistic nature that drew admirers. Edward made a point of going there on Wednesdays when he knew she worked. Her naturally consoling soul was a sanctuary at times for the solo father, and there seemed to be a possible romantic interest signaling to the single father.

"Bucket of balls for your thoughts?" she regularly asked,

Finding Victoria

as her personal greeting to him. Aly brushed back her blondish-brown hair from her eyes. She was beginning to assume a matronly figure, but Edward still found her physically comforting, even attractive.

"Yes, that would be fine, Aly. And how are you?" as he would take out his wallet, although sometimes, with a wink, she would open and close the register without any money or credit card exchanged.

"And how are the girls?" she sipped her tea. From time to time, a group of players would come in and pay for their round.

Edward comfortably recounted the recent anecdotes of his daughters, looking for any kind of feedback on the effectiveness of his parenting. He enjoyed the golf metaphors she injected, saying things like, "At least you're on the green…" and "Concentrate on the shot at hand." There was a sincere appreciation for her interest and casual friendship…moments that mattered to him when there was no special woman in his life. He found her insight helpful, even though she had no children of her own. Her credible life manual was based on growing up with three sisters. More women in his life; Edward couldn't seem to escape them. He truly did belong to the Girls' Club.

Aly eventually suggested they have lunch together one afternoon as a first step toward something more than just casual acquaintances. Although golf can be played alone, there is always more enjoyment when you are with others. Beyond the golf-talk, Edward and Aly discovered they had much in common. The relationship quickly escalated from a 9-hole to an 18-hole in a matter of weeks, and Edward was making quite a few putts.

Despite having the company of a nice woman, with all of its physical benefits, his game still felt off, and things began to feel like he was walking the course without a cart in the rain. But unexpectedly, it was Aly who broke it off, citing she couldn't commit to the shot.

"You are a wonderful man, Eddie," she began. "We have fun,

we laugh, and it's so nice to have someone to walk and talk with…"

"Yes, yes. I feel the same, Aly," responded Edward. Adding, "I think it has been a game of convenience for both of us, trying to dodge loneliness. Fun for a while."

"We can still see each other around the clubhouse," she added, and placed her hand over his. "I don't see beyond temporary passion for the game when we're together."

His daughters were disappointed that their father was alone again. They were old enough to realize that there was a distinct difference between being alone and being lonely, and they wanted to see him have some fulfillment in life.

When his daughters were young, par for the course was the minimum expectation; sometimes Edward met it, and other times he was over by a stroke or two. When Kate came home early from school one day at age thirteen, it was she who had to educate her father about the soiled clothes from getting her first period, after the introduction to menstruation from the school nurse. Despite his ignorance, it was Edward who got the necessary female paraphernalia for her, and he learned to get the stains out of her clothes with a white bar of soap and cold water. Birdie; one under par. And when Rebecca was eight, she had no inhibitions when asking her father where babies came from. What else could he do but tell her the truth? The next day, she started telling her classmates about the word "conceive" and all that it entailed. A parent conference was immediately called. Double bogey; two over par. But when fifteen-year-old Lily took the lead role in the school musical, Edward could not be prouder. Albatross; three under par.

As the years passed, the more he played the game, the better he got. He realized he had teed the shots up for his daughters to the best of his ability. Teaching them to be kind and compassionate when he volunteered at the homeless shelter. He modeled patience and forgiveness when he repaired his relationship with Evelyn, asking her to attend various activities

Finding Victoria

and events in the girls' lives. He showed affection when he embraced them over their triumphs, like winning an athletic event or giving a stellar performance in the school chorus. And he hugged them in their more vulnerable moments: their first heartbreak or not getting an invitation to a birthday party. He shared his silliness in showing off his disco dance moves in the kitchen while cooking dinner; his questionable singing skills as he belted out Motown tunes on the morning drive to school; his good humor in laughing at juvenile television shows. The girls adored him. But despite the joy his triple bogey brought into his life, he was still lonely. He needed companionship and the love of someone who adored and appreciated him as much as his girls did.

One morning several years later, over breakfast, a frank conversation began. Edward's youngest daughter (now an adult) had arrived the previous night on a visit from London. She rummaged through the cupboard for some pans.

"Let me cook you some breakfast," she cheerfully offered and plated a meal fit for a king.

"What's all this?" asked an impressed Edward when he saw a full English breakfast in front of him.

Lily kissed him on the top of his balding head and sat opposite him with her fruit and yogurt. "You're my father. That's reason enough to spoil you a bit."

After the small talk, Lily looked across the table. "When are you going to get on with it?"

Edward looked confounded.

"You're alone. You need a woman in your life. What are you going to do about it?"

"Well, there was Aly," he mentioned.

"Dad, that was ages ago. She was nice enough, but she didn't get you. What can we do here?" Lily queried, as if it were a group project. "They have apps…let's set you up." She grabbed his phone and started punching at the screen.

"I don't want an app."

Finding Victoria

"Well, how about Facebook? You already have an account. There's no pressure."

"I don't know," he said uncomfortably, finishing the last bite of his breakfast. "I'll think about it. Tell me what to do."

In the following weeks, Edward scrolled through dozens of potential dates on his mobile app. It seemed strange coming from a world of face-to-face organic meetings. Instead, he started just searching for people…specific people. He found three old friends from his childhood; he found Evelyn with her photo-filled exuberance. He saw Aly's page: still single. Perhaps that's worth another try, he thought, and paused. But then he searched for Sarah, and after several attempts, he found her. New surname: Blanchard. Part of him felt disappointed, but then he saw that her status was "single."

Do I dare? He thought, and he felt his heart race a little. A thousand scenarios played through his head. She might not respond. What if she blocked him? What was she like now? He gathered as much data as he could from her page. A few group pictures. She was still attractive. Not much else revealed there, and she was not too active on it. Do I dare?, again in his head; he grew even more anxious.

He did it! He reached out. Nothing monumental or risky. Now to wait.

Weeks later, on his sixtieth birthday, his three daughters loaded the car with their clubs, and treated Edward to a weekend of golf at St. Andrews in Scotland. It was a splendid first day. Chambres watched his daughters giggle with delight as they did when they were children. Poking fun at each other, teasing their doting father, and finishing the game with contentment. They walked into the lobby of the hotel afterward, making dinner plans.

"Meet us at the bar at 7 p.m. sharp, Dad," Rebecca called to her father as the triumvirate of women headed toward the elevator together. Edward nodded and pulled out his phone. There was a notification from Facebook. He nearly dropped his

Finding Victoria

clubs when he realized it was from Sarah! She posted that she looked
forward to hearing from him! His adrenaline launched, and he practically floated to the elevator to his room to shower and dress for dinner.

Later, as he sat at the bar waiting for his daughters, the bartender asked Edward how his game went.

And with a smile, he said, "Hole in one, my friend. Hole in one."

Finding Victoria

12 The Fox Whisperer

"Aaaaahhh, evenin,' Commander!" saluted a jolly Richard Stanton, the barman of The Hound & Fox. He reached for the empty pint glass that would soon be filled with a frothy ale for Craig Chanter.

The regular stool-sitter, Chanter, removed his forest green plaid wool cap and took his usual place at the end of the bar. In a graveled voice, that sounded like a pirate, Chanter cheerfully commented, "Fine evening for friends and foes," and then took a deep and thoughtful sip from his freshly delivered glass, as if taste-testing it, even though he had that same local beer nearly every day, Aethelstan ale.

It was relatively quiet at the pub. Chanter recognized the local finance councilor on his soapbox with two town merchants. They were seated in a far corner, in covert mafia fashion, with furrowed brows and emphatic hand gestures.

"What's all THAT about?" Chanter asked Stanton, with a subtle point toward the table with his pint; it was more out of making conversation than of any personal interest.

"Oh, you know Fred Gillow. Doesn't miss a chance to talk about the taxes for businesses on the High Street. Poor Clyde was on his way out as Gillow and Fenn were walking in," replied Stanton as he filled a pitcher. "Gillow's a miserable man. You

Finding Victoria

makin' any big plans for the weekend, Commander?"

Chanter was known to most as the Commander because of his military service, although no one really knew his rank.

"Richard, I honestly don't think too far ahead. Just grateful to be here each day. Never should've made it out of the war. Had that close call in '44," reminded Chanter. He had told the story of his brush with death during WWII dozens of times, but only to those who sincerely wanted to hear it. Richard had heard it involuntarily countless times, given his permanent proximity to the bar.

"I expect I will be on this here stool each night until 7 p.m. as I usually am and then walk myself home to my quiet place and drift off with a snore. No, no real weekend plans," he said, and there was a ring of melancholy in his tone. Outside of The Hound and Fox, he lived the life of a hermit.

"Get you something?" Richard had turned to a young man with shoulder-length hair, perusing the beers on draught. He could not have been much older than twenty.

"Yes, ah, is there something like a local ale on tap you could recommend?" in a clearly American accent.

Chanter chimed in, "Give 'im the Aethelstan," to which Stanton nodded.

"I need two," the assumed American said, holding up two fingers, and then added, "Thanks." He looked over at a small table where his female companion sat and gave the "thumbs up" sign to her. Then he turned back to Richard, "Is it possible to get an order of fries too?"

Placing the pint glasses on the counter, Stanton smirked, "You mean chips?"

"Course he means chips," chided the Commander. "Put it on my bill with the pints."

"Oh, that's not necessary, sir," the stranger said and started to get some cash from his wallet.

"You're not from 'round these parts. Consider it Welsh hospitality. Stanton, I'll take another," he said, holding the empty pint glass in the air.

"That's very kind. Thanks," the young man said to the Commander, as he took his gratuitous libations to the table.

"Hmmm, whoever said Americans aren't polite got it wrong," commented Richard, somewhat amused. There were not too many outsiders in Abergavenny. "Wonder what he's doing here?" He placed a second pint in front of the Commander.

"Oh, who knows what lures people here," said the Commander, who looked over at the young American couple deep in conversation and enjoying their ale. Chanter's wistful expression told Stanton to leave his old friend in his thoughts, and he took the chips over to the table for the American visitors.

"Here are your fries," said Richard, placing the large plate onto the table. "How are you finding the ale?"

The dark-haired woman looked up at the barman graciously with a smile, "It's great!"

"Glad to hear it," said Stanton, and then ventured, "What brought you to these parts? From the States? Most tourists don't find this place too easily. How'd you come to us?"

"Yes, we're from the Midwest in the States. I guess you could say we are doing some research," said the young man who shot a mischievous glance at his companion. "I'm Jamie, and this is my sister, Julia. We looked you up online; we liked the name of the pub. You might say we have a thing for foxes."

Julia nodded, and the two men exchanged handshakes. "I'm Stanton to most around here. Pleased to make your acquaintance," and then added, "What kind of research?"

"Sort of a family history project."

"We're not genealogists or anything," quickly confessed Jamie's sister, as if she were caught in a lie.

"Oh, we get 'genies' here from time to time," acknowledged the barman. "Mostly intellectuals from London. But there are some curious Americans here as well."

"Well, maybe you can help us?" suggested Jamie. He reached

Finding Victoria

inside his stretched, full backpack and retrieved a manila envelope and opened it. It was filled with copies of census records, handwritten notes, and other certificates.

"We're interested in a family by the name of Percy. They would've been in the area as early as the 1700s, but we are looking specifically around the 1860s," said Jamie, with a glint of hope in his blue eyes.

Without hesitation, the response was "Yes, we have Percys by the dozens!"

Julia burst out with an anxious "Really?" She looked at her brother in shared excitement and nearly toppled the remainder of her pint. "We think it's our grandfather's family. He's American, but his line comes from this area."

The barman laughed heartily. "'Tis true we have Percys, but a good many of them have left Abergavenny too. I know some went off to Manchester some time ago…early 1900s maybe? Your ancestors may have been among them. You need to go see Sheila Batt at the town hall. She will know more and can answer some of your questions."

"Thank you, sir," Jamie said graciously.

By the time the Americans finished their drinks and the chips, Chanter had left his stool and undertook his short walk home.

Americans. Chanter smiled to himself, inhaling the cool night air. He had not encountered many in recent years, but then he had not left Abergavenny much either. Two Americans left indelible impressions on Chanter's life, one he knew before the war and the other during.

American Corporal Archer Thomson saved Chanter's life. It was in the spring of 1944 in Italy; when the corporal was fighting the Germans in the Italian campaign, that fate played its hand. The combat had been intense at Monte Cassino. Brits and Americans were aligned in pushing the Germans back from Rome. Chanter found himself in the thick of the first assault on Cassino. He had been knocked unconscious when Thomson

Finding Victoria

came upon him.

"Get your ass up, soldier!" Thomson shouted in encouragement among the fray and chaos. He had seen the blow Chanter took and believed him to be capable of getting himself to safety. But then he soon realized the dire situation, and that Chanter was either dead or knocked out cold.

"Oh, good God," Thomson voiced in his head, and for a brief second, he thought of running from the enemy fire to the safety of his line. But then he looked at Chanter's bloodied head, with streaks of red running down his cheek, and he heard the low moan in the mud. Fight or flight? Instinctive fight kicked in, and the moral code of humanity took over. Thomson stooped to secure the other soldier's shoulders in his grip and began dragging him across the battlefield through sloppy mud and bodies. And then Thomson's human cargo started thrashing; Chanter was waking up.

"Hold on, old boy!" yelled Thomson, who began losing his grip, and then slipped himself into the sludge of war.

Chanter remembered where he was, and, ironically, calmed down. The flailing stopped, and he felt a tug on his shoulders. A voice told him to "hold on," and then there was a sharp pain in his shoulder. A soldier's boot was unintentionally thrust upon it. Thomson had slipped and fallen nearly on top of him.

Then it was Chanter's turn to fight. He turned onto his stomach and tried to get up, but the dizziness prevented him from a full-fledged stand. Thomson screamed, "Crawl!"

And the two men crawled, resembling caterpillars moving among the corpses and devastation. Chanter never forgot the smell of wet mud and blood in his nostrils as they slithered. It was harrowing, but they both made it out, although Thomson suffered some shrapnel injuries later in the battles.

When the war was over, Thomson tracked Chanter down and wrote him a brief letter wishing him well and included a few more details of the aftermath to put his mind at ease. Thomson recalled how he first came upon Chanter on the battlefield, and

Finding Victoria

what they went through to survive that day. The letter was postmarked from a small town called Clio in Michigan. Chanter never imagined the letter might make its way to him, yet it did. A thoughtful gesture. And Chanter made a promise to himself that one day, if he ever had a son, he would like to name him Archer. However, that opportunity would never present itself; the British soldier never married.

But Chanter had been in love…once.

She was an American with a fierce sense of self and long legs. It was before the war in the spring of 1939 outside of a London cabaret called *The Mystic Muse*, in the very early morning hours. Chanter was out for a walk in the cool night air. The climate of change loomed large with WWII just around the corner, but for an eighteen-year-old Chanter, time was at a standstill. He stood at a distance in a London street watching the tall brunette enjoying herself within a small group of young people in their late teens and early twenties when he first saw her come out of the establishment. Her laughter rang clearly above the others. Chanter's gaze went directly to her at the same moment her hat blew in his direction on the opposite side of the street. With several quick steps, he recovered it for its grateful owner.

Holding it out to her, he exaggerated a subservient bow.

She giggled at the gesture and tried to respond with a curtsey but almost fell over in an off-balanced, tipsy two-step. Chanter rushed in time to counter her back to an upright stance.

"Why, thank you, kind sir," she slurred her American accent in the afterglow of an alcohol-fueled evening. Her bobbed brown hair looked a bit disheveled, but she was very attractive even in the dull light of the streetlamps.

"C'mon, Ellie!" urged the group, who had not slowed in their advances down the street.

"Wait!" she called, and she then turned to her knight. "What's your name? I'm Ellen Bowles." "Good evening, rather, good morning, Miss Bowles. I'm Craig Chanter," and they shook hands; hers was a limp attempt in Chanter's firm grasp.

Finding Victoria

Aggressively, she asked with some struggle in putting her words together coherently, "When can I see you again, Mr. Chan-Chan-ner? I'm free for breakfast."

At that moment, one of the other members of Ellen's party had circled back to retrieve his friend.

"Let's go, Ellie," a patronizing, tall, handsome man in an American soldier's uniform grabbed hold of her arm and then turned to Chanter. "Join us if you like. We're looking for a good cup of Joe and some breakfast."

Just as he led his companion away, Ellen Bowles leaned closer to Chanter and playfully whispered, "St. Ermin's Hotel. Room 822." She turned back several times to semi-successfully wave goodbye.

Chanter was enamored. He wanted to see her again.

St. Ermin's was too rich for his blood, but he borrowed a suit jacket for the following afternoon and went to the reception desk to ring Room 822. The crystal chandelier of the main entrance was intimidating enough, but when the doorman greeted him with "Sir," Chanter felt even more out of place. He was merely a groundskeeper.

"Ah, yes, Mr. Chanter," acknowledged the desk clerk. "Miss Bowles is in. I will ring the room now."

And as if spiritually invoked, Ellie came down the staircase opposite the reception area. She saw Chanter before he saw her.

"You came! I thought I imagined you…a dream," she exclaimed, and hurried down the stairs to greet him. "I'm so sorry, I don't recall your name. Was I so terribly intoxicated? We had great fun at the cabaret, although I'm not feeling so full of fun this afternoon," she commented, putting her hand to her forehead.

"What was your poison?" Chanter inquired.

"Gin…God awful," she smirked. "Let's go for a walk. St. James Park is not far from here. Are you from the city, Mr.…?"

"Chanter…Craig, please," he offered his arm as they

Finding Victoria

made their way out into the afternoon sun.

"What is it you do, Mr. Chanter?"

"Gardener."

"A gardener! You grow things!" she said, as if it were the most fascinating profession in the world.

The flirtation accompanied them to the park, where Chanter pointed out the flora and fauna with great ease. He pointed out hollyhocks, daffodil, bluebells, and foxglove, reciting the distinctions among the different types of tulips and explained the history of the bulbs.

"And pelicans!" Ellen excitedly pointed toward the water with the delight of a child.

The leisurely walk lasted nearly two hours, but it seemed to pass in an instant. She became keenly aware of the time and told him she needed to return to the hotel.

"There are foxes in this park, you know," he shared, as if it were some secret.

"Foxes? I should very much like to see them some time!"

"Can you come back here later this evening? Just about dusk."

"Well, yes, I can manage that," she seemed to contemplate as they approached the hotel where they started.

"Fabulous. It's a date, then. Say about 8:30 p.m.?"

She nodded and then hurried into the hotel. Chanter's eyes followed her, and his breath was whisked away with her as well.

Ellen was waiting on a bench in St. James at 8:15 p.m. And when Chanter approached her, he presented her with a stem of purple foxglove that he plucked from one of the nearby park beds.

"How lovely! And appropriate," she said, and much more subdued than earlier, almost coy.

They strolled throughout the park until they came to a small, out-of-the-way area where Chanter frequented. He cautioned her to stand back a bit as he stood ever so still. Reaching into his coat pocket, he scooped out some peanuts and spread them under the cover of some nearby shrubs. Then Craig made some shrill and short shriek-like noises. Ellen did not know what to make of it and wanted to laugh, but she held her breath and froze when she saw two foxes emerge from under the thick shrubbery. Not long after, another one came. Chanter crouched down almost to their level. One cozied up to him like a house cat. But he refrained from reaching out to actively touch them…distant respect was what kept them there. He let them come to him. Ellen's mouth dropped open in awe.

But then a man walking his collie came around the corner, and the foxes scattered in the dusk of the evening as quickly as they appeared.

"Bravo!" said Ellen, with soft claps. "You are truly a fox whisperer! How did you do that? Amazing!"

"Been doing it since I was a boy," he claimed with a shrug, and his companion beamed at him and impulsively kissed him at that moment.

It caught the whisperer off guard, but he welcomed it. She had wanted to do that all day. Their embraced bodies felt like two jigsaw puzzle pieces coming together to complete a picture. A perfect fit…they both felt that.

"Come with me," he took her by the hand and led her to a side street not far from the park where he lived. "Do you trust me?"

"Yes!"

And when he walked her back to the hotel as the sun was coming up the next morning, they stopped a final time in St. James Park where Chanter beckoned the foxes one more time for his new lover in the foreground of the morning dawn.

"My fox whisperer…" she said once again, three words that may as well have been "I love you" in that moment, and she flashed a blissful smile, waving him away before she reached the steps of the St. Ermin. That was the last he saw of her. The great love of his life. The one who got away.

When he returned to the hotel later that day, he found

that she and the party she arrived with had checked out. They had gone back to America as far as he knew.

"Americans…" Chanter sighed to himself, reflecting again on Ellen and Archer's roles in his life. Yes, he loved Americans. His recollections, especially of Ellen, served as a hypnotic serum to send him off to a deep and restful sleep after his evening visit to The Hound and Fox.

The following day, Chanter was pleasantly surprised to see the return of the young Americans to his public place of solitude, and he raised a glass to them from his stool. Richard Stanton noticed them too and made an effort to engage. This time, the siblings seated themselves at the bar, two stools over from the Commander. Jamie had his backpack, stuffed with his family history charts and notes.

"Did you go see Sheila like I told you?" asked Richard to the pair.

They both nodded.

"I'm afraid she was a help in some ways, but in others, it seems, she added more confusion to our research. We almost have to backtrack on what we've been looking for. We'll take two of those Afflestons and some chips," said Jamie with a smile.

The Commander laughed softly from his seat and said, "You mean AETHELSTANS."

Richard winked at the Commander.

"Yes, Aethelstans," confirmed Julia, and her blue eyes met Chanter's with friendly acknowledgement.

The barman hurried off to the kitchen for the order. Chanter was sentimentally interested in the Americans and started some casual conversation.

"What's the meaning of that tattoo?" he inquired, noting a fox silhouette on Jamie's left forearm with the initials E. T.

"Oh, that's for my grandmother. We always had this thing for foxes in my family, ever since we were very young. Kind of like a good luck symbol," shared Jamie. Julia was nodding in agreement.

"When she died, I wanted to do something as a tribute to her," he looked down at his tattoo. "She practically raised us when our mother died."

"Oh, my condolences," the Commander, practically whispered.

"Ever have something keep cropping up in your life but you didn't know why?" asked Julia, who was now looking directly at the Commander. "That's definitely how it's been with the fox. Grandma loved them. Remember, Jamie, your little league team was the Foxes? And my first apartment at college was on Fox Street?" continued Julia.

Richard reappeared and began wiping the bar down. But when he looked at Chanter, who was transfixed in the discussion, he said, "You okay, old boy?"

"Fine, fine."

But then Jamie said something that caused the Commander's heart to react.

"She adored foxes, for some reason. We had fox storybooks when we were little. She loved to tell us the story of the Fox Whisperer. Remember that?" Jamie looked at his sister.

Then the Commander looked at Julia, too. Yes, he saw it now. The hair color threw him, but it was the same smile, the same blue eyes. Even the young man had the resemblance.

"What's your grandmother's name?" the Commander anxiously asked.

Jamie pointed to the initials on his arm, "Ellen Thomson."

"Ellen!" It came out of Chanter's mouth like he had just been given the Heimlich maneuver. And then as an afterthought, he mumbled, "Thomson."

"I'm confused," said Richard, "I thought you were looking for Percys?" He was now curious and invested in the topic.

"Well, we are," confirmed Jamie. "but when we spoke to Ms. Batt today, we hit a brick wall…sort of."

Julia was concerned about Chanter's sudden odd behavior.

Finding Victoria

"Do you need some water?" she asked him.

"No. But I wonder," the Commander posed, "Do you know an Archer Thomson?"

"Of course. He was our grandfather!" responded Julia.

Chanter's brain and heart were working at full speed trying to process what he was hearing, trying to come to the conclusion he could not believe. What are the chances? And was that Archer he met that evening in London outside the cabaret? It had to be. And she married him! He did not want to share this revelation just yet. He sat quietly on his stool to hear more.

Richard turned to the Commander and asked, "Do you know Archer Thomson?"

"Oh, granddad died shortly after the war; you wouldn't have known him. I doubt you've ever been to Michigan," interrupted Julia.

"So, back to the Percys," suggested the barman.

"Well, yes. This whole time, we thought Percy was a surname on our grandfather's side. We had all kinds of DNA analysis and help from others who worked on their family trees. When we shared what we had today with Ms. Batt, she was certain our Percy line was not from our grandfather's line, but from maybe our grandmother's line. But it's not adding up," Jamie took a long drink from his pint.

"We can't find any Percys in Archer's line, but the DNA is telling us otherwise," said Julia, who was still watching Chanter.

"I'll take a whiskey, Stanton," the Commander motioned. He looked a little shaken and frail, like a small gust of wind might blow him off his stool. And when his drink came, it disappeared in a flash.

Chanter looked at the two Americans and then told Richard to summon three more whiskeys.

"You two are going to need to join me for this one," Chanter began. "I knew your grandmother. And I come from a line of Percys."

At that moment, everyone was momentarily confused,

Finding Victoria

except for the Commander.

Richard poured the three drinks. And then he sensed the need to pour a fourth one, for himself.

"What are we drinking to?" asked Julia with anticipation.

"To FAMILY!," cheerfully announced Chanter, who smiled broadly at his company.

And that evening, he told his own version of the story of the Fox Whisperer to his two newfound grandchildren.

Finding Victoria

Finding Victoria

13 Erasing Mr. Corrigan

Love and grief are inseparable and work on a pulley system. Writer Kahlil Gibran described them in terms of Joy and Sorrow: "Together they come, and when one sits, alone with you at your board, remember that the other is asleep upon your bed. Verily you are suspended like scales between your sorrow and your joy. Only when you are empty are you at standstill and balanced."

Queen Elizabeth II gave the most simplistic, timeless, and real definition for grief that I have ever heard after the death of her beloved Prince Phillip: "Grief is the price we pay for love." It was the admission of a wife, not a monarch. And Queen Victoria's palpable grief, after her husband Prince Albert's death, is widely known as she went into mourning for decades, wearing black, and disappearing from public life.

The default association with grief is usually physical death. But grieving comes in many shapes and forms with many causes, and it is sadness measured on a pain level that is off the Richter scale, registering somewhere between a 10.1 and infinity.

This is a story about grief...and love. But there is no cessation of breath, no funeral, no traditional mourning. It's the grief experienced when a loved one fades and ultimately disappears from life due to a neurological disease. Reliable sources point to about one-third of the world's population as

Finding Victoria

victims. But there is collateral damage to their family and friends, so that number is much higher. If you have dodged exposure to it thus far in life, be sure your seat belt is on, just in case.

Dora LaMotte's family did their best to buckle up.

■■

Mr. Corrigan lived in the middle of the street. Growing up in his neighborhood meant being on your best behavior when you were within thirty feet of his property. Children were afraid to ride their bikes on the sidewalk past his house, because if even one blade of grass made contact with the tires, Corrigan seemed to have sensors in his head that rang like a five-alarm fire. Within seconds, he was out on his porch, and, yes, he was that old man warning, "Stay off my lawn!"

He lived in his pristine white house with its manicured yard with his quiet, modest wife. No children. No grandchildren. He cut his grass in his crisp white tank top, thick-rimmed glasses, and scowling face. In those days, men cut the grass in their everyday trousers. His business casual pants with belt made him look like he might be ready to put on a button-down shirt and tie at a moment's notice and go into the office for work. Even his concrete driveway showed no cracks, no evidence of oil drippings from a car (which was kept in the garage with the door closed most of the time), and there were never any tools lying about. He was a mystery to the neighborhood children who paid close attention to him, but no one ever wanted to get too close.

Donald Lamotte, was the only man in the neighborhood who went on the Corrigan property and lived to tell the tale. Lamotte had a Catholic family of seven, including his wife and himself. A lucky number? Perhaps. He never shared what he talked to Corrigan about when he occasionally walked over and rang the bell. Sometimes Mrs. Corrigan would answer the door and smile cordially when Lamotte appeared on the doorstep. Then she would invite him in, and the neighbors would watch and wait. One to two hours later, the father of five would emerge, stoic,

Finding Victoria

and make his way home. Even Lamotte's wife, Therese, was not privy to the details of what transpired during the visits.

One late June Saturday morning, five-year-old Arnold tugged on his father's pant leg and asked, "Did you go to that scary man's house again?"

"Yes, I did," smiled Donald, who settled down to the breakfast table, teapot and sugar bowl in hand. "Maybe you would like to go with me next time?"

At this suggestion, his son abruptly took a few steps back with a mask of horror on his face, and then ran off. Even two of the older children who were already chin-deep into their cereal bowl paused and gazed at their father.

"Isn't he mean? What do you go there for anyhow?" asked Gertrude, the most daring of the children at only age nine. She scooped up the bowl in front of her and drank down the residual milk.

But before an answer was divulged, Mrs. Lamotte, in her green terry-cloth bathrobe, greeted everyone, stretching her arms above her head, grateful for a chance to have had some extra sleep.

"And what are we doing today?" she asked, rummaging through the refrigerator. "Has Silas been up for breakfast yet?" she asked, referring to the oldest Lamotte child, who was fourteen.

"Daddy went to Mr. Corrigan's house again this morning," tattled young Lloyd, who was nearly thirteen and already a clone of his father: tall and thin, legs like stilts. He put his chipped cereal bowl in the sink with a clatter and left the room. Gertrude followed, but not as conscientiously. She left her bowl on the table and wandered off.

The wife and husband made eye contact when Corrigan was mentioned, and Therese Lamotte nodded gently in silent covert understanding. This was not lost on Dora, who entered the kitchen as this telepathic communication took place. The male-female

Finding Victoria

daughter paused as if she had tread into a holy and sacred space that demanded reverence. Therese looked up and asked, "Dora, what're you up to today?"

"I dunno. Maybe play some tennis with Cara," she replied, and then maneuvered in the small kitchen to the pantry to get a box of cereal. "Who keeps putting empty cereal boxes back in here?" she demanded. "I bet it's Lloyd!"

"There are some extra tennis balls in the garage somewhere," Donald informed his daughter.

"Cara always brings a bunch," she said, and sat down to the table with her father, loudly pouring what remained in a box of corn flakes. And then she ventured, "What's with Mr. Corrigan? What do you talk about? He's always so nasty." She stared at her father.

"Oh, he's harmless," started Donald. "He just wants to keep his property in order. Nothing wrong with that."

"Yeah, but what do you talk about?" again she asked.

Therese joined them at the table with her tea.

"Well, Mr. Corrigan was in the service. He likes to talk of his experiences then. Likes to tell stories," Donald smiled at his wife.

"Oh. Sounds boring," said Dora.

"Not too boring. He's led an interesting life," said Donald.

"He doesn't have to be so mean though," Dora said, working on quickly finishing off a bowl of cereal. Shortly after, she excused herself and headed to the tennis courts.

For some reason, that brief conversation stayed with Dora and resurfaced years later when her father was diagnosed with Alzheimer's Disease.

Donald was in the final stages, and life was becoming very challenging. He was at home with Therese, who took on a majority of the responsibility, but had nurses coming in a few days a week. Dora stopped by often.

She had watched a vibrant and active man disappear in the past decade. Her father was becoming invisible. With each visit she tread more lightly, wondering if he remembered who she was.

"It's me, Dad. Dora," she would always cue him. Then she studied his facial expression for any sense of recognition. If she smiled at him, it seemed to help. It certainly couldn't hurt.

If Therese was nearby or in the room, she added some other context before Donald had a chance to think, as if giving answers to an exam. "Your daughter, Donald. She has the two kids: Renny and Macy."

And then some spark of familiarity was evidenced as he smiled gently. Perhaps he knew her or perhaps he was just mirroring the smile she flashed at him.

Dora took his hand in hers and reassured him with a squeeze. "How are you today, Dad?" There was always emphasis on words that reinforced the relationship. And the pause was important. Donald could not be rushed or feel pressured. Dora waited.

He looked confused.

"What did you do today, Dad?" Again, the pause. Again, Therese jumped in a little too quickly and impatiently to answer for him.

"Tell her you went for a walk, Donald," said his wife. And then to Dora, "We went for a walk. He was able to do more than usual today. But we had a tough time getting moving at first. He insisted on putting his shoes on himself and put them on the wrong feet." She gently rolled her eyes but smiled.

The awkward side conversations about a person when they are in the room often took place. Dora wondered if her father was understanding sometimes and just choosing to be an observer. He probably was thinking, "Why do they keep talking about me when I am right here?"

"Walked a bit this morning," Donald commented.

"Great, Dad. What did you see on your walk?" Dora continued, hoping he could connect the dots of thought.

"Went on the boat," her father added. Donald had not

owned a boat for over ten years.

Therese started to correct him, but Dora interrupted and asked, "Who was on the boat with you, Dad?"

"Lloyd…and Dora," he smiled. "Lloyd caught a fish."

"I'm Dora, Dad," she reminded him. "I remember that fish! Lloyd was ten when he caught that."

Donald laughed. "He almost fell overboard pulling it in."

Dora was still holding his hand and excited he was remembering. "We went swimming in the lake, and Arnold got leeches in his swim trunks. Remember?" she chuckled.

Nothing. No expression.

"Who's Arnold?" asked Donald.

"Your son, Donald," insisted Therese. Dora could tell her mother was tired.

"Go rest, mum. I'll keep an eye on him," said Dora.

Therese reluctantly agreed, but she stood in the doorway to the bedroom and just watched to be sure the love of her life was okay before succumbing to the promise of a short nap.

Dora tried to maintain some continuity in the conversation. "Remember the boat, Dad?"

Then the short, truncated responses began to transform into longer recollections as if a clock had been wound inside of him.

"There was a dock at the end of the lake where you kids liked to swim. And a tire swing off to the side. Your mother never liked you playing there. She thought it was too dangerous."

Dora felt the rise of the emotional roller coaster…up, then down, then up again. And just as quickly as the memories surfaced, they submerged again into dementia's murky waters.

Donald stared at Dora. "Who are you? I know you, don't I?" and he was aware that he should know her, yet he didn't. He grew agitated. He withdrew his hand from her grasp. He frowned.

And Dora tried to recover with, "The boat, Dad. Remember the boat?" But she had lost him, and the scrambled memories were on overload. He was shaking his head.

Finding Victoria

"What boat? I don't know you. Stop bothering me," he cried, and he then spiraled into a litany of angry rants.

Therese heard him from the next room and quickly came to the rescue.

"I don't need a nurse," he snarked at his wife, which shocked Dora. She had not witnessed that level of anger before.

"He thinks you're a nurse?" she asked her mother. "How long has THAT been going on?"

"Oh, he gets confused sometimes. One day I am the nurse, and other days I am someone he flirts with," Therese seemed sad when she said it.

"Oh, God, I'm so sorry, mum," said Dora, realizing how much things had deteriorated in a short time.

"He still loves me. I feel it in my bones," said Therese, "He knows I am here for the long haul. That's what matters. For better or for worse. Not going anywhere."

He now scowled at these two important women in his life, and said, "I'm going to call the police. What are you doing in my house?"

"I'm your WIFE," reassured Therese, "It's okay, Donald." She stroked his cheek, and he calmed a bit.

Dora watched as her mother skillfully and compassionately handled her father. A labor of love. Truly.

Therese looked up at Dora and grinned, "Arnold calls him Mr. Corrigan when he gets like that. He had dementia too, you know."

"Who? Mr. Corrigan?"

"Yes. Your father used to go over there to talk to him. Remember? He liked to tell stories, and your father seemed to keep him calm. It gave Mrs. Corrigan a bit of a break. Corrigan really enjoyed talking to your father."

A lightbulb went on in Dora's head. "Was that why he was so mean? The dementia? We were so terrified of him when we were kids. One time Silas ran his bike on part of the grass, and I thought he might wet his pants from the fear!"

Finding Victoria

"Mmmm, yes. The dementia made him angry. But he was particular about his yard even before the Alzheimer's kicked in," Therese said, and then Donald got up from his recliner.

"Where are you going?" asked his wife.

"Have to check on Corrigan," he had associated what he heard and reacted.

Dora called, "Mr. Corrigan isn't home, Dad."

He stopped in his tracks and turned to his daughter, "You kids don't like him, but he is a nice man. I'll check on him later," and he went to sit down again. He forgot that his neighbor had died ten years previously. In fact, the whole family had attended the funeral.

A few months later was the final time Dora saw her father when all of her siblings were at the house for a birthday celebration for their mother. Everyone brought food, and they rented a picnic pavilion for the afternoon. All the grandchildren and in-laws were there. The significance of the moment was colossal.

Donald was confined to a wheelchair, but his wife made sure the outings for "walks" were frequent, even though he did not remember many of them. He smiled broadly as he was wheeled into the midst of the celebration and saw all of his family gathered under the pavilion with streamers and balloons strung across the inside of the roof. The banner read, "Happy Birthday, Mom on your 80th!" in bold red letters. Therese looked tired but beautiful. Her daughters had taken her to the beauty salon that morning while the boys, Silas, Lloyd, and Arnold, looked after their father for a few hours. Hair, nails, the works. She deserved it, her children thought.

"Mom looks great," commented Arnold, who had lost most of his hair. He beamed at his sister, Gertrude. "You girls did a fantastic job."

"Yes, well, it took a lot of arm-pulling to get her to agree to leave his side," attested Gertrude.

"I guess that is what love looks like," said Arnold, and they looked at their parents; both of them were happy in that moment.

"He asked her to marry him yesterday," said Dora.

"What did she say?" asked a concerned Arnold.

"Yes, of course," replied Dora.

"Dad's heart still knows her even if his brain doesn't anymore," said a teared-up Gertrude. The emotions also overcame Dora, who wiped a tear away as Arnold hugged both of his sisters, one under each arm. They were silently communicating their mutual respect and love for their parents. And when their brother Lloyd approached the trio, he instinctively knew what the tears were for and patted Gertrude, who was closest to him, gently on the shoulder.

Donald was not exactly sure of what was happening, but he expressed great joy in being around happy people. Small grandchildren ran by him laughing. A few other family members stood close by with drinks in their hands, telling stories and enjoying themselves. At one point, he looked at his wife and asked, "Are all these good-looking people my family?"

Therese nodded and smiled at her husband, and then wheeled him over to the end of a picnic bench while she went to get him a plate of food. "Keep an eye on him," she said to Silas, who held his infant son in a gentle rocking motion.

"Is that a girl or boy?" asked Donald, peering over at the active baby. Arms were flailing and legs kicking at the air.

"Boy, Dad," said Silas, and he wanted to tell him he had told him that before, but he decided not to.

At this stage in the Alzheimer's journey, Donald often said words that didn't make sense and came out as gibberish. He had no idea what words he was saying, and neither did anyone else. Silas had the least patience with his father, and he sensed an avalanche of the nonsensical about to erupt. He was uncomfortable.

"How is work?" Donald looked at Silas, but not really recognizing him.

Finding Victoria

"Uh, fine…" replied Silas. His wife, poked him.

"You have to add 'Dad' to help him remember," she whispered.

"Work is fine, DAD," Silas reiterated. The baby was getting fussy as if he sensed his father's discomfort. Silas looked around for a rescue offer. No takers.

And then a remarkable thing happened. Donald started to recall incidents from years ago when his children were small. He spilled anecdote after anecdote with great detail and accuracy. The time Arnold won the equestrian trophy, the time Gertrude met Prince Charles, the time Silas fell through the ice and had to be saved by a local farmer. There were still a few gibberish words inserted but the basic gist of each story was coherent. And Donald was Dad again. Mr. Corrigan was erased. Even the inflections in Donald's voice became familiar as well as his animated hand gestures. He could have been speaking Spanish, but his behavior, tone, and expressions were all Donald Lamotte.

The whole family had circled the wheelchair and were listening intently. Even Silas was now laughing over the fond memories his father's brain cache revealed. For some of the grandchildren, it was their introduction to their authentic grandfather.

When Therese returned to the table with her husband's plate and witnessed what was happening, she began to cry, but with tears of heartfelt joy. She could think of no better birthday gift.

Finding Victoria

14 Last Train Out of Bognor Regis

In Nora Griffith's brown leather diary, she entered the outline of a heart around the date August 15. It marked her favorite event of the year, Anniversary Roulette.

The thirty-eight-year-old mother of two had a special overnight travel bag for the occasion. The weathered carpet bag had seen better days with its pug images scattered randomly over its exterior. It was the same one she took on their honeymoon to the States in 2010, and it brilliantly met the sentimental anniversary moment each year. Fifteen years of marriage passed so quickly, and yet it had been a slow dance too. The honeymoon stage ended within the first year when she and Rory lost their first child after a five-month pregnancy. But the despair and emptiness were not long followed by the joyful birth of their round, bald, and jolly daughter, Nicky. And then two years later, an obstinate Spencer was induced two weeks beyond his due date. The extra incubation time was evident as he tipped the scales at eleven pounds four ounces and had a full head of hair.

Nora's husband, Rory, spent much of his time in Westminster on the job with the Metropolitan police as a third-generation bobby, trying to live up to the familial expectations. The career in law enforcement added a few years to his graying

Finding Victoria

hairline, but he felt fit and mentally agile at forty-two years old with a recently retired father and a sharp-minded grandfather still around, Rory felt he had good odds at a long, natural life. It was the unknown influences during the workday that factored more heavily into his mortality that he worried most about.

August 15 was not immediately on his mind, since it was still three weeks away. But when the text came from Nora, it was pushed to the forefront. Rory struggled with the informality of text communication, always careful to dot his I's, cross his T's, and add end punctuation.

> N: we need a sitter for the 15th Can I ask your mother
> R: Yeah, sure.
> N: how many days
> R: 3 or 4?
> N: right, 4
> R: Leaving work now
> N: love you
> R: I love you to the moon and back.

"Anniversary Roulette…" he mused aloud as he shut down his computer for the workday.

"You two STILL doing that?" his longtime partner and best man, Ollie Grayson, snickered from the nearby desk. "Seems a little risqué to me. I would never be able to get Laura to do that."

"Well, maybe that's why you and Laura are sleeping in separate bedrooms!" and before Grayson could reply, Rory was out of the office.

The tube ride home from Westminster was usually uneventful packed, and quiet. If Rory was not in any rush to get home, he would linger in Victoria Station to get a cup of coffee from Nero's, have a guilty pleasure snack of dark chocolate, or browse the latest books in Waterstone's. Then he would board the short

Finding Victoria

Tube ride to Clapham High Street Station, only a few blocks from home. Sometimes Nora and the children would meet him at the station so they could all walk home together. That was when Spense and Nicky were small. Now, as budding adolescents, the children were too occupied with their phones and too embarrassed to be seen with a parent in public.

"Mmmmm…what smells divine?" asked Rory, entering the kitchen from the short walk home. Nora enjoyed experimenting with meals, so there was always guesswork in figuring out what she was cooking.

"New recipe," Nora replied, holding out the wooden spoon for him to taste. There were quite a few splashes of red sauce on her Fortnum and Mason apron from her enthusiasm over the stove.

"I think there's some ginger in whatever it is," said Rory with his face over the skillet.

"Very good," clapped Nora. "You get seconds. How was work?"

"Nothing noteworthy. Ollie is jealous of our anniversary plans. Did you call my mother?"

"Ollie has no sense of adventure, and neither does Laura for that matter," Nora remarked. "Your mother can come watch the kids."

"Perfect. I have the time off from work."

"Really looking forward to it this year. It seems special… fifteen years," she reminded him.

Rory sensed that maybe he was obligated to put some extra effort in this year. Nora's "special" comment hung over him like a storm cloud. Fifteen years. In today's world of marriage, that was quite an accomplishment.

When the anniversary morning finally arrived, Nora was running late trying to organize the children for her mother-in-law. Rattling off reminders that were unnecessary to recite and pointing out where the dog food was among her other frenzied comments.

Finding Victoria

"I know, I know," assured Mabel, Rory's mother. "Grab your bag and get going now! We'll be fine. You'll never get out of here at this rate."

Rory came down the stairs with a sense of calm. He had made all the pre-arrangements for a special holiday, no matter where they ended up. He set his black bag in the hall and kissed his wife. "Let's go," he whispered.

They took a taxi to Victoria Station, as the excitement and anxiety were building for Anniversary Roulette. The rules of the game dictated that they would each choose a number, one through eight. The first number would be the number of the train schedule board, beginning from the left. The second number would be the number counted down from the top of the destinations on the designated board. Then they would board for that location. Spontaneous.

The couple stood in front of the train boards with the crowds but did not look up at them just yet.

"I say three," said Nora confidently.

"I will go with five," added Rory.

Their eyes together scoured the boards to determine their anniversary destination.

"Platform 10!" exclaimed Rory and pointed, as if he had won the lottery.

"And five down, makes it…Bognor Regis!" laughed Nora. "Oh, God…what have we gotten ourselves into?"

Even though each was a seasoned traveler within the country, neither of them had been to Bognor Regis. They knew it was on the southern coast. Once they got on the train, Nora started voraciously researching it on her phone.

"Oh, that takes some of the fun out of it," Rory scolded. "Let's just see what we have when we get there." Meanwhile, he was doing his own internet research in preparation for their "special" celebration now that he knew the destination. He was contacting a hotel, a florist, some restaurants for reservations, and a jewelry shop. All the things a good husband should do.

Nora agreed to put the phone down and watched out the window as church steeples and cows sped past the English countryside like a flipbook. Despite the less than two-hour ride, the humming of the train on the tracks lulled her into a brief nap. When she awoke, the train was slowing. Rory nudged her, "We're here, darling!"

Only a handful of passengers were getting off at Bognor Regis. Passengers filed out the door and looked around. The station was relatively quiet.

"Let me check on trains home," said Rory to Nora, and he approached an official at the station.

"How often do these trains run back to Victoria?" Rory inquired.

The uniformed man looked carefully at Rory and Nora. "They run every two hours. Mind you, you'd best be sure you are on the last train before sundown or you'll encounter muggers and molesters! Or worse!"

Rory looked anxiously at his wife, hoping she had not just heard what he did.

"Whaaaaat?" cried Nora. The conductor nodded his head to reiterate his point.

"It will be fine," said Rory. "We're here for a few nights, and we can take an early train back in a few days." He took Nora's arm and led her away from the platform and through the station to the street.

"We've never had any problems before with locations. Do you think our luck has run out here?" asked Nora. Above their heads was colorful bunting that read, "Bognor Regis: It HAPPENS here!"

"I've got an address for the hotel. Let's get a taxi," instructed Rory. He was in charge of orchestrating the details of the anniversary each year.

But when they gave the driver the address, the mustached driver turned and gave them a frown. "This is not a street I would take even my ex-wife to! It's not a safe place. I have a friend who has rooms not far from here. Let me take you there instead. She has fair rates." He paused for their response.

"I say we do as he suggests," immediately said Nora. And before Rory could enter his vote, Nora told the driver they were on board for the new destination.

It was a quaint and well-kept four-room bed and breakfast. No other occupants were there, but the woman who ran the place, called Sam, was pleasant and friendly.

"What brings you to the Bog?" she asked, serving them refreshments in the small kitchen. "Help yourself to some biscuits or scones," and she set a plate in front of them with some jams. Then, before she took a seat at the table with them, "Get you a cuppa?"

"We're celebrating our fifteenth wedding anniversary," proudly said Nora.

"Yes, and we seem to be off to a rough start," chuckled Rory. He had already changed the delivery address for the flowers and balloons to surprise his wife.

"Oh, how wonderful. Congratulations. Been married myself four times, but none lasting as long as that," she remarked, helping herself to a heapful of jam for her scone.

"We saw the beach within a short walk from here. Do you have any recommendations on what we should see while we're here?" asked Rory, glancing over at Nora, who seemed to have settled since the change in plans.

"If you're into trees and the like, there's Hotham Park. Only a few minutes from the beach," Sam suggested and then added, "But I'd stay away from it after dark."

There was the warning again about after dark.

"We'll venture off to explore in a bit. Thank you so kindly for the tea," said Rory after a few minutes of chit-chat. He stood from the table to gather the bags.

"Oh, yes," said Sam. "Here's the key to your room. Number two, top of the stairs. Dinner will be served promptly

Finding Victoria

at seven o'clock if you are interested. It is included."

"Oh, thank you, but we have a reservation for our anniversary dinner at The Marble Faun," said Rory. Nora smiled at him, knowing she had a delicious meal to look forward to.

"Marble Faun, you say?" asked Sam with a strange expression.

"Are you familiar with it?" asked Rory, now a little concerned.

"Oh, yes. The food is excellent, but it attracts a seedy crowd at night. But judge for yourselves. I rather like the roast beef myself. Well, enjoy yourselves today." Sam left them to their room and plodded back to her work in the kitchen.

"What do you suppose she meant by that?" Nora pressed her husband. He only took a few things out of her bag and placed them in the drawer.

"Oh, I don't know," dismissed Rory. "It had great reviews. And they serve fresh seafood."

"It's only noon now. We have time to spend at the beach and maybe the park afterward. Then we can come back here to clean up before dinner. How does that sound?"

Rory folded down the bed sheets and gave a seductive stare. "I think we have a little bit of time for a short anniversary warm-up round before we go to the beach?" He patted the mattress, Nora coyly slipped into bed, and they began their intimate rehearsal for the real play that would come later that evening.

The rehearsal ran a little longer than they planned, but neither was complaining.

"Two o'clock," said Rory, after their post-tea tumble. I have a couple of small errands I need to take care of, and then let's get our suits on and hit the water," Rory sprang from bed. "You can relax here and take your time until I come back." He kissed her on the forehead, got dressed, and made his way down the stairs.

When he returned to his wife, they explored the beach,

Finding Victoria

where the crowds were thick. Tourists and locals swarmed the food vendors that lined the sand's edge near the main road. Crying children could be heard, barking dogs, and the shrill sound of seagulls filled the air. The warm sun pierced their skin as they held hands, walking along a path between the sand and the road where some modest houses overlooked the sea. Children waded into the water cautiously. A few sailboats in the distance floated against the seascape.

At one point, Rory paused on the walk and pulled Nora close to him, embracing her like they were newlyweds. "Fifteen years," he breathed. "I wouldn't share that with anyone else," and he kissed her on the tip of her nose. "Perhaps we'll settle down here in our retirement and live in one of these houses that overlook the sea?"

Nora laughed. "But what good would that be if you can never go out after dark?"

"We don't need to go out after dark," he teased and then patted the curves of her behind.

"Now, don't you start," said Nora, who was enjoying every minute of the attention her husband was giving her.

They asked a passerby if he could take their picture. It was part of their Anniversary Roulette requirement. One day, they could share all the annual photos with their children...all the places they had been together on August 15.

It had been a blissful afternoon of walking and swimming, sunning and laughing, relaxing and loving. When they returned to Sam's place at 6 p.m., a police car was parked in front. The local constable appeared stern and unfriendly. He was speaking to Sam, who was gesturing and shrugging.

"Oh, here are the lodgers now," said the temporary landlady, beckoning the couple to approach.

Nora and Rory seemed confused, but they obliged. "Anything we can help with?" asked Rory, casually shaking the sand out of his shoes.

Finding Victoria

"How tall are you, Mr...." began the officer. Nora noticed he had a fresh mustard spot on his clean white shirt.

"It's Mr. Griffith, and I'm six foot even," offered Rory.

"I'd say he fits the description to a tee," said the officer to his partner, who stood next to the car. "Should we take 'im in?"

"Might be best to make it official. Where have you been today, Mr. Griffith?" asked the first officer, turning again to the couple.

"Been to the beach most of the afternoon," started Rory, and then decided he need not mention the afternoon seduction of his wife, although this man might need a racy story like that as a highlight to his day.

Nora was fumbling a bit with her sandy beach towel and biting her nails.

"Happen to have been to any jewelry shops today?" inquired the policeman.

"Well," Rory said, then stopped and looked at his wife, trying to avoid ruining the anniversary surprise. He had bought her a diamond pendant for their anniversary at a small shop in town.

The officer noted the pause and made the executive decision to bring Rory into the station. "Let's get you to the station. I think you may be able to help us out, Mr. Griffith."

"What?" said an astonished Rory. "Is that entirely necessary? I am an officer myself, you know."

"Badge?"

"Uh, well, no. I haven't packed it. I'm on holiday. Our anniversary," Rory said, and wrapped his arm in proud territorial fashion around Nora's waist.

"Well, she can come along too, then. Let's go," directed one officer while the other started the engine.

Rory and Nora got into the backseat in bewilderment.

"Rory, what is happening?" whispered Nora once they were in the car.

"I'm not quite sure," Rory responded; he held her hand.

Finding Victoria

"Clearly there's been some kind of misunderstanding here," she softly said, but loud enough for the driver to hear.

"We'll get it cleared up," her husband assured her.

They were led into an interrogation room once they arrived at the one-cell jailhouse not far from the train station. Paint was peeling from the walls, the furniture was well-worn, and the light fixtures were outdated.

"It smells in here," said Nora. She was growing frustrated, but she took a seat. It was their anniversary, and this is how they were spending it…in the Bog jailhouse!

"Now, how's about telling me about the jewelry shop, Mr. Griffith?" asked the officer who had been asking all the questions earlier.

"I went in and purchased a gift for my wife. That is all," he confessed. "Can we leave now?"

Nora lit up and smiled.

"Well, you see here, Mr. Griffith, that shop was robbed this afternoon, and well over £400,000 worth of jewelry was taken! Your description was provided by three witnesses."

"Yes, I was there, sir, but as I said, I bought my wife a pendant necklace and I only spent a fraction of that amount. I have the receipt," Rory started digging through his wallet. "Yes, here it is!" He held up the paper in triumph.

The officer took it and looked it over. "Hmmm, receipt for one pendant necklace with two diamonds. Cost £549."

"See," commented Rory defiantly.

Unsatisfied still, the officer asked a few more questions before releasing the couple.

"And you didn't see anyone else there? What time exactly did you leave the shop?"

"There were two others in the shop: a well-dressed man with grayish-blond hair looking at engagement rings and a young red-haired woman in a green paisley skirt having a watch repaired," Rory recalled. "The man was about my height and a bit on the heavy side. The woman had a tattoo on her left forearm. I think it had the image of a beehive or something. And the shopkeeper was there too, of course." His cop experience made him an excellent observer of people.

As the policeman noted the descriptions, Nora was bubbling with excitement to get her anniversary gift.

"Is there anything more you need from us? Can we get a ride back to Sam's?" asked Griffith.

"Of course. We may need to follow up with you later, if you don't mind though."

When the Griffiths returned to the bed and breakfast, Rory gave an exhausted glance at his wife. "We've missed our dinner reservation. Shall we call it an evening? Perhaps we can have some of whatever Sam cooked up?"

"Can I have my gift now?" smiled Nora eagerly. There was no shame. The woman loved her jewelry.

He reached into his pocket and produced the gray velvet box and flipped it open. A grateful wife tightly hugged her husband and whispered, "Thank you" in his ear.

Then she said something he was not expecting. Nora said, "Let's go home!"

"Now?"

"Yes, now. We've missed dinner. We have been to the beach. This destination has not been much of a holiday; we spent part of it in a jailhouse. I've seen enough. I am fine with just going home now. It was a lovely anniversary, darling," she said, admiring her pendant. "I love you. I will cook you up something delicious tomorrow, and we can have a quiet celebration at home." She seemed neither upset nor disappointed, just in a space of quiet acceptance that things had not turned out as planned. Rory felt the same.

He chuckled, "All right. We'll be home by ten if we leave now. Let's pack up."

There were some questionable characters at the train station, some shady beggars among them. Nora noticed the dirty trash that had collected in the recesses of the building. She clutched her purse against her as if pickpockets lurked around every corner. They had been warned, after all, about being in the Bog after dark, and the daylight was waning.

Rory was just anxious to get home. There was quite a large contingency of travelers who were also eager to get out of town. It was the last train out, and the nightlife in the Bog was surely something to be avoided.

Then the herd collectively made their way onto the train with the warning bell clanging in the background as Rory and Nora breathed a sigh of relief, stepping into their car and finding a seat.

Once the sounds of steel began and the gentle rocking of the ride commenced, Rory fell asleep. Nora looked around at the full capacity of the car. There was a family of five with tired and sugar-overloaded children…messy hair, rumpled clothes, but contented expressions on their faces. Across the aisle was an older woman in a large sunhat with her small Yorkshire terrier sniffing around for a treat. A group of rowdy middle-aged men had already started a card game and were dropping f-bombs within earshot. And a couple was sitting adjacent to them. It was the red hair and the tattoo on the woman that caught Nora's attention. There was a glittering gemstone bracelet on her wrist. The man beside her unbuttoned his formal suit jacket to reveal a bloated tummy, and he eased back into his seat.

They matched the description Rory gave earlier of the people in the jewelry store. Nora looked over at her peacefully slumbering husband and decided they had had enough excitement in Bognor Regis that day and kept her observation to herself.

Maybe next year they should retire Anniversary Roulette?…she thought. Sometimes there's just no place like home.

But maybe they would break protocol and return to Bognor Regis the following year to see what happened after dark!

Finding Victoria

15 "And the Award Goes to…"

"I feel like Loretta from *Moonstruck* when she is getting a makeover to meet Nicholas Cage at the opera!" Florence Bennett announced, admiring herself in the salon mirror. She was pleased the gray hairs that had inched into her brunette life at fifty-four had gone back into pseudo-hibernation.

"She meets Ronnie, not Cage, at the Met," corrected Deb, the stylist, who stood behind her client, teasing and blowing out the last few sections of hair.

"Well, you know what I meant…Cage's character," conceded Florence. "Now all I need is that gorgeous red dress and shoes!" She recalled the scene in the movie when the lead character, played by Cher, walks the streets of New York the morning after spending the night with Cage at the opera, and kicks a can nonchalantly down the road.

"I've never been to the opera. Have you, Flo?"

"No, but I could listen to Puccini all day," sighed Bennett like a schoolgirl with a crush. She started humming Nessun Dorma from *Turandot*.

Finding Victoria

"Okay, lady. You are Loretta for another eight weeks, and then we'll do this again. Go find your Ronnie!" teased Deb, who now examined her own hair in the mirror, considering a change.

"Thank you, Deb," waved the transformed widow of fifteen years. Florence had only recently started indulging in clothes, travel, exotic cuisine, and manicures and facials. She even started buying brand-name groceries over the generic brands. Her two children were grown and on their way to budding careers and homes. It was time for her; she finally relinquished long-held responsibilities. She worked hard most of her life, so why not?

But she was also acutely generous and visible to others. She had entrenched herself in community service to find purpose after her husband passed away. Running meals to the homebound and sorting clothes at the local thrift shop to benefit the local branch of the cancer society, these activities filled her days. Everyone in the town knew her. And, everything she was involved with was infused with her real passion: the movies!

From a young age, Flo was a film junkie. No genre was off limits. She could precisely quote a line from a John Wayne western as well as any iconic remark from a James Bond film. And she was a connoisseur of children's movies, with *Chitty Chitty Bang Bang* and *Willy Wonka* as her favorite subjects.

"The hair in the Gene Wilder version is just terrible! I don't think they had money for stylists on that film," she would tell her children when they were growing up and sharing a viewing.

"Pretty harsh, Mom," her daughter would criticize in response.

"Roald Dahl must've wanted a whiskey when he saw how dark that movie is…especially the scene in the boat where Wonka states in a frightful sing-song tone: 'There's no earthly way of knowing… Which direction we are going… There's no knowing where we're rowing… Or which way the river's flowing.' Or how about that long-nosed man who rounds up the kids and puts them in cages in *Chitty Chitty Bang Bang*? What kind

Finding Victoria

of children's films scare the Dickens out of them?" she always brought up.

February and March were the highlights of her year: the BAFTA and Academy Awards ceremonies! She held wine and cheese gatherings with elaborate charcuterie boards and tables and required formal dress. She one-handedly boosted the economy of the rural town of Malmesbury during this time with people buying new attire, women making appointments for hair and nails, not to mention the increase in liquor sales. It grew to such popularity that she rented out the town hall for these celebrations, complete with a big screen.

And Flo knew her audience. Rom-Coms she reserved for the salon talks with Deb. But with her enthusiastic gardener, Charles, it was always historical dramas. WWII and Nazi discussions wafted in the summer afternoon over the mulching of the fragrant roses and the snipping of the dead-heads of the hydrangea.

"How scared do you think Schindler was?" Bennett posed to the perennial expert on *Schindler's List*, as she handed him a cold glass of lemonade in the summer heat of the garden.

"Fear?" asked a surprised Charles, wiping the sweat from his aged brow. He stood up with the pruning shears in hand. "There was no time for fear. His moral instincts took control. Once that happened, there was no going back. There was no choice."

"I don't know if I could be that brave," Bennett doubted, shaking her head, considering the risks Oskar Schindler took in employing Jews in his factories to spare their lives during the Holocaust. "So many people risked their lives for others. Still, even Schindler insisted, 'I didn't do enough." But what IS enough?"

Charles paused from his pruning task, "I suppose there is never enough when you are saving others. Someone always needs to be saved."

"Someone always needs to be saved..." she echoed. "True. So true," agreed Bennett.

Finding Victoria

And they carried on, with Bennett following three steps behind her green-thumbed friend around the garden, hopping then to other movies: *The Zookeeper's Wife* and *The Book Thief*...all part of their Friday routines and discussions.

Florence found that the vicar of the local church was a closet admirer of horror, which always made her smile. It was their little secret. These discussions took place far beyond the chit-chat that commonly occurred outside of the church service as people exited the pews on Sunday. Monday mornings, she often met Reverend Liam for a coffee or tea at the café beside the rectory, where there was also a small souvenir shop to raise funds for the current historic abbey that dated back to the 12th century. It was known for the flying monk who supposedly flew from its tower on homemade wings. It was a quiet venue and home to their guilty pleasure, resembling a Hollywood movie set.

"What of the coincidences surrounding the making of that film? Can it be cursed?" inquired Florence, "Surely that cannot be part of God's plan?" They were analyzing *The Exorcist* in hushed tones. Reverend Liam excitedly leaned in as if they were engaging in something of an M16 nature.

"No, indeed. It's devil's work, of course," he told her, referring to the fire on the set that burned everything except the bedroom of actress Linda Blair's character, injuries to some on the set (including the star of the movie), and even a murder committed by one of the actors.

"Do you think people who watched it were affected by the spirit of evil? For goodness sake, moviegoers were vomiting and fainting in the theaters!" Flo recounted. "When I saw it, I could not sleep in my bed with the lights out for months!"

"Some people are more susceptible than others to evil, but I also think the power of suggestion may have been at work in those cases," the reverend offered in an effort to bring the temperature down a bit.

Finding Victoria

"What of exorcisms? Do those really happen in this day and age?"

"Oh, yes," began the reverend, and he told her of an exorcism done by a Catholic priest in a nearby town a decade earlier. Flo wanted to hear every word…

Every conversation Flo had contained a movie reference and, rather than people being annoyed by it, it fascinated them with the catalog of knowledge she had. She almost served as a walking movie trailer for the film industry. When Flo was having an exceptionally social week, ticket sales at the local movie theater coincidentally rose. This was a phenomenon that could not be refuted. Her Christmas cards even showcased an image from holiday movies with some humorous speech bubbles inserted, like the split-screen image of the delightful Sebastian Cabot version of Santa from *Miracle on 34th Street*, juxtaposed with Dan Ackroyd's smelly drunk Santa from *Trading Places*. The text read "Before Christmas" and "After Christmas" respectively.

If she had lived longer, she might have been something of a social media influencer or podcast hostess. But one quiet evening, while watching a movie, one that wasn't even a blockbuster or an award winner, Flo Bennett took her final breath. She was caught up in the dystopian science fiction film *Soylent Green* with Charlton Heston; she had seen it many times. No one would ever know she left this world at the scene where the elderly man, Sol, goes off to his death at the Thanatorium. It was a depressing scene, but the room for discussion over that would have been great, for which Flo would have approved.

The morning of Florence Bennett's funeral, the town was flooded with visitors and residents. It reminded one of the diverse gathering at the end of the movie *Big Fish*. There were several brief but touching and respectable oral tributes presented, but it was the final one given by a man of small stature, in a formal mourning suit with ascot, who approached the lectern. Flo would have likened it to the somber nature of

Finding Victoria

the character in *Four Weddings and a Funeral* reciting the W. H. Auden poem for his deceased partner.

There were murmurs among the pews of who this man was, and he disappeared immediately after the eulogy without a trace. No one recognized him, which was odd for the small town. With speech in hand, he cleared his throat and began:

"Many of you came here today to honor Florence Bennett; you've arrived by **trains, planes, and automobiles** and some just on foot. In remembering **my fair lady** today, I hope to turn your hearts **from grief to gratitude**... thankfulness for a woman who meant so much to all of us.

Before Flo makes her **exodus** from this world to the next, let me share with you this woman's **lust for life** and her exquisite gift for building bridges between people so they are **strangers no more**. She was truly a **giant** when it came to bringing people together.

As you are all aware, her passion for film and connecting it to each of our lives was not a **mission impossible** for her. She had the uncanny **sixth sense** to identify what made people tick, what ignited their **soul**.

You may have observed her among a group of **women talking** at the farmer's market on **the theory of everything** from the **sound of music** in movies to the soundtrack of our lives, conjuring memories of our first kiss to family car rides. Or perhaps you overheard her discussing **the human comedy** at the butcher's shop while waiting in line with the other customers. She might playfully recall incredibly bad slasher films as the "thunk" of Mr. Garvey's cleaver could be heard behind the counter. Even though some people might think that was in bad **taste in the afternoon**, most would erupt into conversation by sharing their favorite horror films. Even in the **dead of night**, Flo was known to be firing off a few emails or texts to friends or family with encouraging words or confirmation through film references that these were indeed **the best years of**

Finding Victoria

our lives despite any hardships and that *the pursuit of happiness* should never be abandoned.

It was her wish to make it *until September,* so that she might see one last *change of seasons*. And as *a river changes course*, she wanted for you to re-examine your life and leave no one in it *unforgiven*, fight for love with the fury of a *raging bull*, and be the *golden compass* to others who need guidance when life gets *rocky*.

If Flo taught us anything, it's that *it's a wonderful life.* Our time together on earth is but a *brief encounter*, and *from here to eternity, the greatest showman* will provide a beautiful *place in the sun* where we all may gather again for a matinee or two in our *days of heaven*."

And then a strange event occurred. Everyone in the church stood up and applauded for what won, in their minds, in the Best Eulogy category. And though a standing ovation seemed sacrilegious inside of a church (outside of a wedding), Flo would have loved that for an ending. And there would be discussion about the mysterious man who gave the final eulogy…

Finding Victoria

16 "I Think That I Shall Never See…"

Everything about ten-year-old Lionel Bamford was fragile, especially his ability to connect to others. He was the middle child in a family of five and the runt of the litter. From the beginning, Lionel faced challenges in life. Ill health followed him from his birth. He was an early delivery and on the cusp of being considered a premie at thirty-seven weeks, five pounds and four ounces.

Ian and Marian Bamford were expecting a third girl when Lionel surprised them. Mrs. Bamford carried the baby wide around the middle, which her grandmother insisted was a girl. The same look she had when she was pregnant with her first, Jillian, and her second, Bridget. There was no preparation done for a boy. Ian felt like Henry VIII waiting for his heir to the throne to finally arrive, so he was secretly extra pleased with the news. He had his boy; no pressure for future additions. The family was joined by a fourth child, another girl, Stephanie, and finally another boy with Aaron.

Lionel proved to be more work than his siblings through no fault of his own. He remained in the hospital longer than the others simply because he was not physically ready to make his debut to the world yet. He needed time to grow. The Bamfords took turns visiting him in the ICU until he was ready to go

Finding Victoria

home. It was like patiently waiting for bread to bake in an oven.

The doctors had told them Lionel might be a little slower to develop, and they should not hold him to the same standards and milestones compared to the other children. He would come along in his own good time. So, when Jillian and Bridget were taking their first steps at ten and eleven months, respectively, Lionel celebrated his first steps at fourteen months. First tooth, first word, first solid food…they all came a few months later than his siblings for Lionel. It was not mentioned, just understood.

But as the children grew older, the differences began to bubble to the surface because Lionel's siblings noticed and were vocal. And the comments were not always encouraging not supportive: "How come Lionel gets to have a special teacher at school?" "Why doesn't Lionel have to take the swimming test?" "Why do you like Lionel better than me?" or "Why does HE get extra time?"

The middle child himself recognized he was a little different from his siblings. His parents knew early on there might be a chance of some cognitive issues, but they remained optimistic. However, the signs became more clear that the older Lionel got, he had his own gifts and deficiencies. Doctors mentioned "slight autism," "on the spectrum," and "25th percentile" for growth.

Sometimes reading skills, particularly interpretation, were a challenge; but analysis for math calculations and science was more astute than anyone three to five years older than him. His coordination in physical activities was still lagging. Once, when his father took him to the golf course to learn how to drive a ball, Lionel took a swing and the club cut loose from his hand and struck another golfer in the back, which required a trip to the hospital. Another incident occurred when he was fishing and hooked his own eyebrow, which cost him four stitches. Making friends and feeling a sense of belonging to a group was also difficult, even with four siblings. Sometimes he uttered inappropriate things in the company of others, like when he asked his grandmother what size bra she wore at a church function or announced at the dinner table that his parents slept in the nude. It often created awkward situations for the Bamfords.

Despite these impediments, Lionel thrived. His great passion was for nature. And in an environment filled with plants and animals, it was when Lionel was at his best. The Bamfords fostered this in him from his earliest days. Pets were ever-present in the household. There were hermit crabs, cats, dogs, hamsters, rabbits, birds, and even a ferret. Only once did a large snake cohabitate, but that ended when the hamsters started disappearing. And when most parents have to nag their children to feed, walk, and clean-up after their pets, these parents had a child who was always willing and able to do these tasks voluntarily without having to be told, which is a rarity.

One morning at breakfast, when Lionel was ten, Marian mentioned to her husband some concerns she had with the pets.

"I love that Lionel looks after the dogs with such commitment, but he needs to give the others a chance to show they can be responsible too. Bridget hasn't walked the dogs in over three months. And when I asked Jillian to feed them, she had no idea what to give them or how much."

"I see what you are saying," her husband agreed. "Why don't I give Lionel some other things to focus on, like the garden. There's plenty to keep him busy out there with weeding, watering, trimming…things I hate to do."

"Great idea."

And it was. Lionel abdicated from his animal kingdom and joined the Green Thumbs Club. A master gardener in the making. The other children were unhappy about the new arrangement because it meant they had to pick up the slack, but Ian was quietly relieved to hand over some of his own responsibilities. Lionel felt like he was getting a chore promotion.

"Now you don't want to overwater these," Ian told his son,

Finding Victoria

pointing to the flower beds. "And if you start to see any white spots on this, let me know right away."

"What about the fertilizer? Shouldn't we be adding something to the dirt to help them grow better?" asked a serious Lionel, who sounded more like a plant nursery owner at times than a child.

"Well, yes," said Ian, who was awkwardly caught off guard and knew nothing of soil. "Something you can research, Lionel." It was Ian's standard line when he had to backpedal out of his ignorance: "Something you can research." He used that line with all of the children. Marian used it herself a time or two.

Lionel was a hybrid of a sponge and data recorder. No details got by him when it came to anything that had leaves, stems, fruit, and chlorophyll. He was a garden prodigy at age ten. So, when he had to choose a topic for a speech in school, there was no doubt it would focus on his newfound love, plants, and in particular, trees.

Marian worried about the project when Lionel first told her about it. "He's scared of his own shadow when he's not in the company of plants or animals," she said to Ian.

"You know, he's got to overcome this social anxiety at some point, Marian. Everyone goes through that, not just children who are…" he stopped short. Marian hated it when anyone labeled Lionel.

"I know, you're right. But the kids can tease so mercilessly sometimes. He's never had to stand up in front of a group before speaking about anything. And he's only ten," Marian took on her motherly worry tone.

"He can practice in front of us. We can record him, so he sees himself. He'll enjoy that. How long does the speech have to be?"

"Four to five minutes. No more, no less."

"Fine, we'll get a timer on him. Has he said anything more about it?"

"No, but he must be terrified," Marian furrowed her brow,

and then exaggerated, "He might be scarred for life!"

"Hardly. I'll talk to him about it after dinner," assured Ian.

Later that evening, Aaron, the messenger, had stuck his tongue out at Lionel when he announced the invitation to their father's study. The chair in front of the desk in the study was reserved only for those in trouble with their parents. Bridget had spent the most time in that chair over the years, but Lionel rarely. He begrudgingly took the seat in front of the desk. He wondered why he might have been summoned to be there and loudly plopped into the swivel chair, expecting the worst. It was the equivalent of being called to the headmaster's chamber.

Ian took his place behind the desk. He always felt that it established a visceral power role in any scenario when he had to discipline his children. His own father had similar props, but those also included a paddle. However, this was one instance where punishment was not part of the equation. He looked at his obedient son, and he second-guessed why he had called him into the study at all; it was under false pretenses. But there was no other private place in the house, save the loo, to have a conversation. And that would only be under desperate circumstances.

"You're not in trouble," began Ian. Lionel was rotating the swivel chair back and forth in his fidgeting, with his feet barely touching the floor and his butt on the edge of the seat.

The chair froze. "I'm not?" asked Lionel, who looked at his father with a mix of relief and confusion.

"No, not all. I wanted to talk to you about your speech for school."

"Oh, that."

"Have you decided on a topic yet?"

"Yes. I want to talk about trees."

"Trees?" Ian considered. "Yes, I think that's a fine choice for you."

"I don't think the class will like it."

"But YOU like it, and that is what matters most," Ian

Finding Victoria

said, but in the back of his mind, he was thinking his son was correct in being concerned about the audience. Why would ten-year-olds want to hear about trees? Especially on the level that Lionel was certain to propose. His speech might be better suited for a room of environmentalists.

"The teacher told me to choose something I was interested in, so that's what I'm doing."

"What exactly do you want to tell your classmates about trees?" Ian was very interested to hear the response to this.

"About how much I love them!" said Lionel proudly.

This was a surprise. Ian expected a litany of scientific facts and statistics to be rattled off or an explanation of what the formation of the rings meant…hard facts, which Lionel excelled in. This was an entirely different direction.

"I see," said Ian, intrigued.

"But I want to do it on my own," he asserted to his father.

"No help…at all?"

"No, sir," Lionel seemed determined in this.

Ian made the hard call later with his wife that there was to be no interference in Lionel's preparation for his speech.

"I mean it, Marian. And don't give me the sad look of a mother who just wants to help her son," he smiled. "He can do this."

There were ten days until Lionel had to present his speech, and during that preparation time, he could be observed carefully memorizing and rehearsing with mumbled words to himself as he walked around the house or worked in the garden. Or he would be seen sitting at the kitchen table writing furiously but covering his notes when someone wandered too close. The family was dying to know what the exact content of the speech was going to be, or at least Ian and Marian were, with the older children taking a mild interest.

"When are you going to practice your speech for us, Lionel?" asked Bridget one day. "Have you memorized it yet?"

"I'm not going to do it in front of you until I've done it at school," Lionel said.

"But aren't you going to be nervous?"

"Why would I be?"

"I don't know. All those eyes just staring at you, and if you mess up, everyone will know," teased Bridget, hoping to instigate trouble.

Marian overheard this and scolded her daughter. "Stop putting pressure on him!"

"I've been practicing in front of an audience," he said.

"Who?" asked Marian.

"The trees, of course," he said, and went out into the garden.

Bridget looked at her mother and made the gesture for crazy with her finger in a circular motion.

Marian was worried but bit her tongue as promised.

The morning of the speech, there was kinetic energy throughout the household, and Lionel got lost in the shuffle. The chatter included talk of the field hockey game that Jillian had after school, the history exam Bridget had, Mr. Bamford's appointment with the dentist, and a host of other activities and events that were to take place. Even Marian had not acknowledged this was Lionel's speech day until she dropped him off at school. This was probably for the best. No one needs an overprotective mother stirring the emotional pot.

"Good luck, darling," she called as he exited the vehicle.

Later that afternoon, there was a phone call from Lionel's teacher. Marian braced herself, but she was on the verge of tears with joy when she was told, "Your son is remarkable!"

And when he came home, and the family asked how the speech went, Lionel simply said, "Fine," and went about his business in the garden.

What he did not know was that the teacher videotaped the speech and shared it with Ian and Marian. They were amazed at what they viewed.

They saw a very confident and poised boy share his passion for trees in a speech that began with some description of types of trees, an explanation of how trees were beneficial to the planet, and it ended with a poignant recitation of the poem "Trees" by poet Joyce Kilmer. He was even smiling and pausing at the appropriate times.

"I think that I shall never see a poem lovely as a tree… A tree that looks at God all day, and lifts her leafy arms to pray… A nest of robins in her hair… poems are made by fools like me, but only God can make a tree." The words floated off Lionel's tongue, and it was Ian who had the tears in his eyes when they listened to the recording of Lionel's voice and watched his measured demeanor, making eye contact with all of his classmates.

"Those children didn't even laugh or snicker when the words 'breast' or 'bosom' were mentioned!" remarked Marian.

"Ten-year-olds don't know what a bosom is," laughed Ian as he wiped his eyes. They both decided it was the most beautiful poem they had ever heard.

That speech became the launching point for Lionel's life journey that helped him connect with others and instill his sense of place in the world. Every major decision he made moving forward could be traced back to the speech. He studied plants; he became a researcher looking for plant-based medicines and cures. He was blessed with awards and accolades for his work. He traveled the world, made friends, had a family, and lived a respectable life. His parents could not be prouder.

Decades passed. And it was no small surprise when Lionel took on a volunteer job at the local arboretum in his retirement at age sixty-seven. The anonymity of the position involved little stress but a great deal of social interaction. As the official mascot of the arboretum, Lionel transformed himself into Theo the Tree. It involved a full-body costume made of foam and plastic that resembled the caricature of an animated tree. His responsibility? To greet people and walk through the park, helping visitors learn about the trees and answer their questions. His enthusiasm was legendary even with the adults. People

Finding Victoria

looked forward to seeing him. It was a treat for everyone. He could share his passion. He often recited Kilmer's poem to the delight of visitors. The words had become a part of his soul. The arboretum even started using lines from the poem in ads.

One day a woman asked, "Why is your name 'Theo'?"

Lionel thought about the poem and said, "It means 'Gift of God.'"

"I like that," said the woman, and they shared a moment.

Finding Victoria

17 Come to Jesus Moment

Seventy-six-year-old John Tottey was a line-crosser. He did not see black and white borders on anything, only blurred, gray edges. "There are always exceptions to the rules," he would beam. But there was one exception to his own rule, no gray area when it came to his wife, Maura, and their marriage.

So, when she asked her atheist husband to go with her on a spiritual retreat of sorts, it was natural for her to question her own common sense. After fifty-two years of marriage, there was nothing outside the realm of possibility when it came to John. He was as unpredictable as a baby's sleep habits.

"What exactly will we be doing at this Jesus convention?" he humorously asked her, but he was open to the idea because it meant a great deal to his wife.

"It's not a Jesus convention," she laughed. "Just a bunch of good people getting together to explore spirituality. It's not even just about Catholicism either." Maura came from a strict background of priests, sacraments, the rosary, and terrifying confession. She added, "Might be good for you."

"Will there be food?"

"I would imagine so if we are going to be there for three days," replied Maura, still unsure if he would commit to going.

"There's not going to be campfires and Kumbayah

Finding Victoria

sing-alongs, are there?" he posed in a more serious tone as he looked across the breakfast table at Maura.

"No. It's mostly seminars. We can sign up for whatever we like. I have the list here if you want to look at it. We're not talking about sweat huts or anything like that. It's at the convention center, for goodness sake. How off the wall can it get?" She slid the brochure over to her curious husband. "Now that we are older, haven't you given any further thought at all as to what comes next?"

"You mean heaven and all that?"

"Yes, I mean 'heaven and all that.' I don't know about you, but I do plan on walking through the pearly gates."

"I know. You and Saint Peter will be chatting away like old friends when you get there," he smiled. He was opening the brochure. "It's a nice thought. Heaven. Maybe THIS life is heaven, and once my last breath has been exhaled, I just start the process of becoming part of earth's compost pile? That's it."

"You aren't going to change this old Catholic's mind about heaven, dear. You know that. But I may be able to change yours. See anything interesting in there?" Maura was encouraged by his examination of the brochure.

John studied the listings and read a few titles aloud, "'*Walking on Water:* An in-depth analysis of miracles from a scientific perspective.' Now, that might interest me," he said in earnest, and then continued to read. "*'Paganism's Hold on the 21st Century.'* I guess that one speaks for itself."

"There are all kinds of religions addressed and focused on too, love. Mormonism, Islam, Buddhism…there's even one on African tribal religions," remarked Maura, who was clearing the dishes while they talked.

"And why do you want to go to this again?"

"I'm going for the ones dealing with the scriptures, but I want you to go to the ones that interest you. We don't have to go to everything together. There are three sessions a day, but two are fine, and we can wander off and get a bite to eat or

Finding Victoria

just relax at the hotel. It will be fun to go into London; we haven't been in so long," she told him, offering her concessions.

John knew he would agree to go from the beginning, but he let her play out the bargaining. Usually, they landed on an acceptable compromise. He felt like he was getting closer to it. There would be time away (like a mini-holiday), a nice hotel, no driving, good food, a happy wife…and perhaps he would enjoy some of the seminars.

"I guess I can stomach some Bible-thumping and prayer for a weekend," he agreed, and she came over from washing the dishes to kiss him on the cheek.

"Just be on your best behavior," she cautioned him in half-jest. She knew how he loved to challenge people on their beliefs, especially their religious views. Being an atheist made it easy for him.

His grin gave away what his wife knew would be an interesting weekend.

Maura planned to meet several of her Bible study group friends at the convention center for the event. The morning she and John arrived, there were some already there at the ExCeL Center. Some brought their spouses, partners, or an adult child. There was some surprise on Maura's part when she saw her friend, Joel, who was a Catholic deacon. His sister, Belinda, who was well into her sixties, was accompanying him. From what Maura could remember, the sister had married a Muslim.

"She's a convert…knows a lot about religion in general," whispered Maura to her husband.

"Even converts are here to get in touch with their beliefs…be born again, understand the Koran, eat some good food…" John teased.

"It's just that she's pretty private about her beliefs," Maura mused. "Surprised she's here," she added.

Joel could see the expression on Maura's well-lined face. "You remember my sister, Belinda?" he re-introduced.

"I'm just here for Donnie Osmond," she admitted.

Finding Victoria

"Oh, yes, well, there's that!" chimed in another of Maura's friends who was giddy like a teenager.

"Donnie Osmond?" asked John, who seemed to be a little intimidated over this fact, and stood a little taller and puffed his chest out ever so slightly to avoid overt detection. He was like a male bird or animal subtly defending its mate.

"Yes, he's one of the keynote speakers. I think for tomorrow. He is representing the Mormon view," informed Maura, who started to primp her hair and pinch her cheeks for color. "I would not mind getting an autograph. He's still as handsome as ever!"

"You'll have to get in line behind ME, then," warned Belinda.

Who knew women of their age would lose their minds over a '70s heartthrob, John thought. But he was just content that Maura was enjoying herself. Marriage was about compromise and sharing, something they had been successful at since they first met. But he must admit, Donnie Osmond did look good for his age. Maybe he should be envious?

The friendly group dispersed, and Maura and John made their way to the registration table, and walked away with their goody bags of assorted items. John rifled through his with the fervor of a child going through their Halloween loot. There were magnets promoting various churches, the usual ink pens, a string of rosary beads, coupons for meditation sessions, a bookmark with spiritual quotes, candies, and even an eraser in the shape of Jesus. John pulled out a bumper sticker and held it up. It read "Say a Prayer for Mother Earth."

"Who sponsored THIS?" asked John.

"No idea, but I like it. I'm putting that on my car," Maura said. "Now, which session do you want to go to first? I'd like to attend the one on saints."

"Hmmmm, I'll pass on the saints. I'll sit in on the *'Getting Close to God Through Meditation.'* The doctor said meditation might help my blood pressure. Wouldn't hurt. Let's meet back here after," suggested John. He was sincere in his interest in the meditation.

"Okay. See you later," and Maura blew him a kiss as she wandered off to meet Saint Peter and company.

The meditation seminar was filled with over fifty people, prepared for about thirty. John stood in a tightly packed room along the back wall. The speaker began with a depressing personal anecdote about a tragedy-riddled life that led her to meditation as a remedy for her challenging life.

John looked at the woman next to him, who was highly engrossed, and commented to lighten the mood, "She'd be better off just going to a Happy Hour!"

The woman was not amused, and she wriggled her way toward the front of the room, away from John.

The speaker discussed different techniques and wanted to lead the group in a short exercise. "Now, everyone, close your eyes," she instructed, and then intentionally paused in silence.

John took advantage of the quiet and commented aloud, "Hands to yourself, people." A few quiet bouts of laughter followed, but the speaker redirected with, "We need to take this seriously, if we are to clear our minds."

The atheist played along, but he found it impossible to calm his racing thoughts. He focused on his breathing but got distracted when his stomach started growling. The perfume of the woman next to him was overpowering, not in a good way. He thought he heard nose-whistling. A jet was flying overhead and could be heard through the closed window. The room was getting warm. John opened one eye. Most were floating away with the instructor to a land of peace and quiet. But one young man was scrolling on his phone, a woman was filing her nails, another person was writing down some notes, and yet another was rummaging through her purse.

John decided he had had enough but waited for a transitional moment to exit stage left. And it came when everyone was told to find a partner. In the shuffle and murmurs, John slipped out. He still had over an hour before he had to meet Maura.

Finding Victoria

The main hall was filled with people from all walks of life, many different countries and cultures, and all ages of adults. It was a truly beautiful mosaic of harmony in the microcosm that seemed to diametrically oppose the macrocosm of economic sanctions, energy source disputes, natural disasters, political power struggles, and more in the outside world. John liked the feeling here. What he didn't like was a hot room packed with people with no sense of humor and those who were trying to come to terms with their inability to relax.

He followed the signs that directed the crowds toward a food court area; he was on a mission to soothe his vocal stomach. And it was on the escalator that he believed he found Jesus.

Coming to the bottom of the moving stairs was like opening your eyes and finding yourself in Munchkinland. A tall, Jesus-like figure was standing at the bottom blessing people, complete with beard, white robe, and brown leather sandals. And John knew something was not right when he peered behind Jesus and saw Luke Skywalker wielding a green lightsaber in swinging motions over his head. He was not in Kansas anymore, and maybe the spiritual convention was just a dream. There should have been a sign that said, "Do not adjust your set," because the cast of characters only increased in number and scope. Mickey Mouse, the Power Rangers (all except the red one), Naruto, Superman, Wonder Woman, Deadpool, Poison Ivy, and ones that were so bizarre, John could only stare.

The lost man finally grabbed Spider-Man and asked, "What is THIS?"

"Comic-Con, man!"

"What's that?" asked a confused John. He noted only a few civilians in the crowds.

"You don't know Comic-Con? Fans of comics, cartoons, science fiction…it's a convention. You dress up, dude. Meet your heroes." And then he disappeared into the busy background of the convention that butted up squarely with the spiritualists at the top of the escalator. This place was like the

Finding Victoria

underworld, John thought, and he laughed at the ironic absurdity of it, because a devil character then walked by, waving to people with his pitchfork.

Looking at his watch, he calculated about an hour before he had to meet Maura and made an easy decision to drift here among the true spiritualists. This was fantastic, he thought. There was an open Q&A stage with stars from recent blockbuster science fiction films, and John stood to observe for a while. He recognized some of them. The fans clapped with fury and excitement when they were introduced.

There were significant giveaways at booths for trips, costumes, books, autographed glossy 8 x 10s, t-shirts, and anything Comic-Con.

"How much for the raffle?" John asked, pulling out his wallet.

A character who looked like a distorted version of Spock from Star Trek told him, "Twenty pounds. You are eligible to win ANY of the prizes. We draw winners every hour."

"I'll take two," said John, swiping his card. He tucked the two tickets into his pocket and moved on. He had no idea how far the festivities went. He wanted to see more.

People were getting their pictures taken in the Batmobile. John was game and struck a serious pose with his arms crossed behind the wheel. Twenty-five pounds. He swiped.

"Who are you supposed to be? Uncle Grandpa?" asked a teenager in a Princess Peach outfit from the Mario Brothers game who approached him. She was accompanied by a Pikachu.

"I don't have a costume," he laughed.

"Uncle Grandpa. It's a character. You look like him. Can I get a picture with you?" she raised her camera to take a selfie. John gave a toothy smile. It was clear he was enjoying himself. He looked at his watch. About twenty-five minutes left. And he still had not gotten anything to eat.

After pushing through the thickening crowd, he found a small sandwich vendor called *Psycho Psandwiches*.

Finding Victoria

"Care for the Norman with four meats, or the Mrs. Bates, which is vegetarian? Ten pounds each," asked the vendor who was dressed in a bloodied apron.

"I guess I'll take the Norman," replied John. Swipe.

He took his sandwich to a quieter corner of the hall where some tables were spread out. Some people were eating, and others were simply taking a break from the sensory overload. He closed his eyes momentarily and just took in the atmosphere without the visuals. It smelled like a buttery movie theater. There were sounds of muffled voices coming from microphones, a streaming of intermingled conversations echoing in the vastness of the hall, the rhythmic steps of people who walked by his table, video game sound effects, and other miscellaneous audio emissions. But then it went quiet, and John experienced a sense of calm. A few minutes went by.

"Hey, mister, are you okay?" a woman who looked like Wilma Flintstone was tapping him on the shoulder.

"What? Oh, yes, thank you," John said, opening his eyes. "Just resting my eyes."

Wilma seemed convinced and then walked away.

But what really shook John was the realization that he had just cleared his mind and was meditating! It was exciting to him. However, he did not revel too long, because he realized he only had less than ten minutes to get back to Maura, and he was not sure how far he had distanced himself from the escalator back to heaven (or hell, depending on one's perspective).

He was on the move, and he knew he was on the right track when he saw the raffle stand. Coincidentally, they were reading off that hour's winning numbers. John paused and took out his tickets.

"5-6-3-3-2-1" read the loud voice over the speakers.

"Oh, my God! I won!" exclaimed John, and he went to collect his prize. The prize was quickly dispatched into a large shopping bag, and the winner happily trotted off to meet his wife.

Finding Victoria

With the sounds of Sodom and Gomorrah behind him, he returned to the land of piety and blessings. And there was Maura, right where they agreed to meet.

"I thought I had lost you to a cult or something," Maura teased. "How was the meditation?"

"Great!" answered John, who was telling the truth as it applied to his experience downstairs.

"Really?" with some surprise in her voice, "What's in the bag?"

"Oh, just some things I picked up," was all he said.

His wife knew he would tell her eventually. "Don't you want to know how my session went?"

"Of course. What saints did you meet?"

"Well, I didn't meet any because the speaker canceled. By the time they told us, it was too late to attend another session," she said, but there was no disappointment in her voice.

"Oh? So, what did you do for the past hour?"

"I explored. Then I went down the escalator, and let me tell you, I found Jesus!" she smirked and did the sign of the cross.

John looked at her with as much affection as he did in their early days of dating, and said, "I found Jesus, too!"

They each said it so loud that people passing by were convinced this was a couple truly touched by the Holy Spirit.

"How badly do you want to go to the next session?" asked John.

Maura shrugged. She had been tainted by the touch of Comic-Con.

John opened the bag, and she peered in. "Oh, My!" was all she said, and then, "John, we're crossing lines here."

Her husband asked, "What do you say?"

Maura nodded and said, "I'm ALL IN!"

And their next appearance at the convention center was in full costume; John was in a cowl and cape as Batman, and Maura had a whip in hand with her black spandex attire and cape as Batwoman.

Finding Victoria
It was the most spiritual experience they ever shared.

Finding Victoria

18 Fish & Chips and Warrior Therapy

Divorce is the Ninth Ring of Hell in Dante's Inferno, especially when it has been forced upon you and you have no say in the matter. I have friends who tell me that there are "good" divorces. There is no such thing.

One Sunday morning, my wife, Ava, and I were having our quiet coffee, whittering on about plans for the summer, possibly a trip to Spain.

"…Yes, we could spend a few days in Majorca. I haven't been there for years…" she nodded, loudly stirring her morning elixir of high-octane Columbia Dark Roast and cream.

I began rattling off some other places we might visit. The beaches of Portugal, a cruise to Greece, a river boat down the Rhine.

Then she drew in a deep breath as if preparing to sack a longtime faithful employee, and simply said, "I'm not in love with you anymore, Tom; I want a divorce."

There is no weapon of mass destruction more powerful than that declaration: "I'm not in love with you anymore." Rejection at its purest. If warring countries throughout history had an arsenal with the potential to be as soul-crushing as these words, there would be permanent global peace.

Finding Victoria

I consider myself to be a reasonably strong person emotionally, but in that moment, I became another innocent victim at the Heartbreak Hotel and had no idea it was coming. The sensation that my stomach was exploding and my legs were taken out beneath me was what I felt first after the numbness wore off. Throw in a samurai sword slice or two somewhere.

I knew that look and the tone of hers. There was to be no argument, no period of negotiation. And to add insult to injury, she added, "I just can't do this anymore," and she got up from the table. No eye contact. Somewhere down the hall and in my heart, a door closed…slammed.

When I replayed that breakfast scene in my head later (no fewer than two hundred times), I tried to determine if this was an act of cowardice or bravery in her manner of announcement. I dissected, analyzed, probed…months afterward, I concluded it was decidedly cowardly and petulant. She made the decision without any consultation and declared the end to our marriage as if she had decided she did not want dessert after a meal. After all, she would have to defend her point and hear my rebuttal, which was what she was trying to avoid. It's called a "discussion" where you both talk, you both listen, and then you both come to a decision. I was angry. The Captain's monologue from *Cool Hand Luke* echoed in my head, succinctly summing up this "failure to communicate," which would become the foundation of most therapy sessions. I was devastated, but later I was bitter. I was many things. People say there are five or seven stages of grief, but it feels more like twenty. Mostly sad.

The days that followed were uncomfortable and strangling. To share a home with someone who just rejected you is torturous. My mother once told me, after my father died, after over fifty years of marriage, that she could bear the grief, because some things in life hurt more; "rejection is far worse than any grief," she said. I believe her now.

Finding Victoria

There were comings and goings in the next couple of days. Rushed packing and emotionless purging. I observed Ava's "piles" of her life sorted: her things, my things, and those shared, yet to be decided. There was very little actual conversation, only short mutterings between us. All civil to a degree. Cold. Painful. Unhelpful.

"I'm taking this," she said, holding up a well-traveled black garment bag. She stuffed some dresses into it.

Taking it *where*? I thought.

She moved out after a few days. "I'm staying with a friend," was the generic comment when she left. I made one weak effort to engage before she went out the door.

"Aren't we going to talk about this?"

"Not right now, Tom. I need time." The door closed.

There were a few texts from her. Mostly just checking on mail and letting me know she was fine. No "I love you" or "I'm coming home," which is what I wanted to see. It took nearly another week, but later I discovered she was with Louis Radford, the local jeweler in town. My neighbor, Wanda, unknowingly let the cat out of the bag while we were walking our dogs together. I took a few days off from work to get my head on straight. Wanda and I talked about the separation as we headed toward the trail leading to the meadow. She was a thrice-divorced middle-aged woman with the bloom still on the rose, and she seemed content with her quiet life just outside of Bath with her dog, Winnie.

"I am so sorry, Tom," she said as she took her whippet off the lead, who then happily pranced across the field. "I saw Lou pick her up, and he helped her with her bags last Thursday."

"Last Thursday?" I was confused because that was over a week ago; today was Friday. The big blow had come over coffee just five days prior. Gears were turning in my head at sonic speeds.

"Yes, I am certain, because I was taking the trash bins out."

Finding Victoria

My Sherlock Holmes deductions shouted the obvious, but somehow my rational brain failed to connect the dots. But before I could manage the conclusion, Wanda said it for me.

"You don't suppose Lou is the 'friend' she is staying with, do you?" She casually tossed a stick out to Winnie, who seemed disinterested.

"Mmmmm," I murmured with some expression of rejection of the idea. "We've known Lou for years. I buy all my jewelry from him. Ava has been in there to pick things out. He's been to our house for dinner."

"So."

"Well, maybe? I am sure he was just trying to help her out."

"Helping her out and having her stay with him seems a bit extreme to me," suggested Wanda. She then threw the stick to my terrier, who attacked it with vigor. "I think he's fancied her for years."

The wheels were coming off the bus for me.

"You mean they are *together*?" The idea seemed impossible, yet that's what a betrayed heart does; it lies to us.

"Tom, just ask her…when you two can start to really communicate again. You can't control what she thinks or feels right now. Focus on yourself. You don't even know what you did wrong."

"This coming from a woman who has been married three times," I laughed. "I don't know if that makes you a credible advisor or a complete fool."

Wanda cackled at the friendly accusation. "I have learned a few things, I suppose. But, what is consistent in all of the marriages is that I should have expressed my feelings more and tried harder at making things work…there are solutions if the lines of communication are open. And even though two of my marriages ended on my own prompting, I wholly regret letting all of them go without much fight. Find out what she wants… and what she expects from you. Twenty years of love shouldn't be thrown away so easily. Lou is probably just a distraction, an

Finding Victoria

outlet for things that are really bothering her. You are a warrior. You'll make it."

"Okay, Wanda…you're not such a fool," I smiled.

Waving to her as I went up my driveway, I could feel the buzz of my phone from the inside pocket of my jacket. "SIMON" lit up the screen. An old school chum. I answered.

"Simon!"

Out of laziness, I switched him to speaker-phone and went into the house, setting the phone on the kitchen table. Looking for any evidence that Ava had been there, I was disappointed to find there was none. Just emptiness.

"When are you coming back to the city? Missed my chips this week," he teased from the tabletop.

Simon and I made an effort to meet up a few times a month for lunch in London. I took the train to Victoria Station three days a week to my mundane job with Remington Data, working remotely the other days. If you are looking for the best fish and chips in the city, there is a small café tucked away on Regency Street, a few blocks from the station and not far from Parliament. Its plain black tiled exterior beckons me, and I answer the call with Simon regularly. It's the office where my old friend and I solve all of the world's problems and leave satiated.

"Yes, well, chips…we have much to catch up on," I admitted.

"Nothing serious?"

There were no secrets with Simon. "She wants out."

"Ava? What are you saying?"

"The D-word. She's already packed up and left."

"That's tragic, mate. What prompted that? You coming into the city tomorrow? I have to run now, but let's talk more. Meet at noon? Usual?"

"I took the past few days off, but I'll be in tomorrow. Will see you then. Noon then. Goodbye."

"Cheers."

Finding Victoria

The train ride seemed long, with my thoughts jumping from one scenario to the next concerning my wife. "What ifs" played out in rapid succession like the rhythm of a machine gun. Simon would provide some point of view or option that I would not have considered. He was always good for that. Level head. Optimism. Steadfastness.

Victoria Station was atypically subdued when I got off the train. There was already a queue forming in front of the café when I turned the corner of Fynes Street toward the familiar smells and sounds. I stepped up behind a bulky fellow in a black biker jacket with the words "Climate Warriors" in sprawling gold letters on the back, with a graphic of planet Earth on fire underneath. This made me smile, not so much for the message it implied, but because Wanda had called me a "warrior" the day before. In contrast, his female companion had on a t-shirt that read "Fly Now, Pay Later." Just goes to show that opposites do attract, I guess.

Simon was punctual to a fault and was seated inside. He texted, "I have a table. Skip the queue!"

I was going to be THAT person, skipping the queue, and started my entitlement walk to the café door, avoiding eye contact with those who had been waiting ahead of me. One elderly woman with a cane and sharp tongue accosted me by putting her walking stick in front of me, barring me from continuing on.

"There's a queue! Starts back there," she pointed with her empty hand, keeping the stick firmly in place in front of me.

"Terribly sorry," I fumbled nervously and pointed to the window. "I've a mate waiting inside."

She seemed doubtful, but then, after projecting a scowling look, reluctantly allowed me safe passage. This café was serious business, and its clientele was unrelenting and territorial.

Simon held a hand up as I entered. He always liked a back corner table, claiming it as the John Wayne seat…back to the wall, full view of the room. In contrast, I preferred to look at as

Finding Victoria

few people as possible, especially because I felt like I was wearing an invisible "L" for loser on my forehead for all to see.

"The queue is maddening," laughed Simon, sipping his Earl Gray. "I got your flat white. Still hot." He slid it over to me.

"Been awhile," I said, looking around. I missed this comfort.

"Now what's this dreadful business with Ava?"

Simon's interest was sincere. He seemed to have a very loving marriage with his American wife, Bernie. They had overcome mountains and molehills to be together. Surely, he had some words of wisdom that I could benefit from.

"She left, Simon. Fed up. Point of no return. Nada. Finito," I shrugged. "I think she's been having an affair with the jeweler in town. My neighbor seems to think so anyhow. I'm starting to believe it's true." Suddenly, reality was settling in again, and a swell of nausea overwhelmed me. Rejection…worse than a death.

"How do you know?" asked Simon.

"About the affair? It's just starting to make sense, and the neighbor saw him pick her up with her things."

"Did you talk? Ask questions?"

"She didn't give me a chance."

"Give her some space. The grass is not always greener. Some people sort that out on their own. You need to focus on yourself right now."

"Yes, well, what the hell am I supposed to focus on exactly? And how much time am I supposed to give her?"

Simon always preached "Absence makes the heart grow fonder," when things got tough in a relationship, but I believed in the line that followed: "And makes it easier for eyes to wander." My wife had wandered, while I lived in a fantasy world where everything was unrealistically perfect.

"At least a few weeks. Let's get some lunch," Simon had a mammoth appetite but never gained weight. I followed him to the order counter with sullen circumspection.

Finding Victoria

Halfway through the meal, after hashing and rehashing my predicament, Simon said some things I had not expected.

"Here's the most important question. What will you do if she wants you back?" he asked.

"What?" I was confused. We skipped a few steps.

"You heard me. What will you do?"

It seemed almost too hopeful a prediction and impossible in my mind. I knew this woman. She had decided. That was it.

Simon waited for my response.

"I don't think that is going to happen," I started. But part of me grew excited at this possibility. Could it even be possible? But then, no. I could not torture myself with that. "I can't get my hopes up, Simon."

"Is it getting your hopes up? Are you really going to want her back after this? Betrayal is a tough one to bounce back from. Can you walk that road with her? Can you trust her again? You've been hurt. You'd risk that again?"

"Well, I…"

"Your relationship will require more work than ever before. Are you prepared to do that? For HER? For YOURSELF?"

"I don't know."

"So, start seeing the world without her in it. You have no control right now over her or her role in your life. Move on. At least explore what it looks like without her. Did you ever think maybe there's another plan for you?"

"You mean like God?" I asked. "I didn't know you were a religious guy, Simon."

"Mmmm…no regular church attendance, but I think there's - something bigger than ourselves at work. Perhaps some master plan…things work out the way they are supposed to. Look at me and Bernie. There's not a chance in hell we should have worked out, but we did. Don't get me wrong, our paths went in different directions for a while. Something brought us back to each other. Later, there were sacrifices. Bernie left her home to live here, but sometimes in life, you just eventually have to go for it."

Finding Victoria

"So, what are you saying?"

"Just give it time. Look inward. Be still. And let her go…for now. See what develops. Work on yourself. Date if you need to."

"That's it? No fight? No communication? Live with this pain?" I was visibly angry. This was not exactly the advice that that I was expecting.

When I left Simon at Regency Street, my heart and steps were heavy heading back to Victoria Station.

For six months afterward, I woke up every morning wondering if this might be the day…the day I was not in pain. For God's sake, I was forty-nine years old and feeling like my first sixteen-year-old crush broke my heart, only multiply that twenty-fold. I was functioning, but as if I had a toothache that would not subside.

I started going to the gym regularly and eating better. Work seemed less of a burden. Purging things from around the house made me feel better, too. Each week I was dropping off items either to the local thrift shop or charity warehouse. One day, while I was going through some old boxes, a passage from a book I read long ago surfaced. It was from *Way of the Peaceful Warrior: A Book That Changes Lives* by Dan Millman. It must have inspired me at some earlier point in my life, but I had since forgotten it. I read it as if for the first time, and some phrases jumped out at me.

"Love is the only reality of the world…Release your struggle, let go of your mind, throw away your concerns, and relax into the world…do your best. Open your eyes and see that you are far more than you imagine… Wake up, regain your humor. Don't worry, just be happy."

Truth when I most needed it. Finally. I put it on my refrigerator to read every morning. My new mantra.

Reinventing myself would take some time, but it was possible. I felt a need to help others, give back. It redirected the focus away from myself. It helped me to feel needed again. Trying to plug a hole. A very wide and deep hole.

Finding Victoria

I even started training for a marathon. It was called The Raging Warrior Marathon in Somerset. I figured it was a sign. I felt more like a warrior in recent weeks. Nothing was going to set me back or keep me down. My neighbor Wanda even came to cheer me on and took me out to dinner to celebrate finishing.

But sometimes, when I allowed it, I still felt something missing. Her. But life went on, of course, as it does; it just continued to be different. I tried to avoid thinking of us.

There was little to no contact from Ava. I did not even run into her around town. There was word she had left the area for a time with Louis. I reached out a few times with inquiries related to household bills or other household management types of things. I only got curt texts or very esoteric emails. No calls. And to be honest, I was astounded at how a person could cut another out of their life so quickly, so sharply after such a close relationship. But there you have it, one of life's wonders. Clearly, she was living her best life and was happy. I did not even know what that meant anymore. Happy?

I was emotionally walking precariously on a tightrope. Trying to balance a new direction where I was alone and independent, and one where I still deeply loved my wife and wanted to be there if she needed me. If there was ever a purgatory, this was it.

Becoming more social was something Simon encouraged. He invited me to his place for dinner once every fortnight. Sometimes, he introduced me to single women he and Bernie knew. I wasn't ready for that quite yet, but I finally went out on a date with a woman named Rita. She was tall with straight blonde hair, and age was sprinkled on her like a fine mist. Her gray eyes reminded me of my wife, and her figure was a little more curvy; I felt open to getting to know her better. She seemed quite taken with me, which was Viagra for my ego.

Dating in your twenties is a different animal than dating in your forties or fifties. But we went to dinner, and all that polite and baggage-free freshness was nice. Attention, interest, flirtation…it was all there. And, yes, physical attraction…or maybe it was need, possibly desperation. There was no coyness when I walked her home. She invited me in, we had a drink, and we fell into bed.

It was more basic carnal instinct than anything. There was an awkwardness in navigating at first. She wasn't Ava. And I had not been with another woman in over twenty years. But how much could sex change, really? I was unfamiliar with the program, but part of that made it exciting. There were things I missed though…but mostly I missed the way it felt to be with Ava. I wasn't really ready for this, even though my male instinct was reacting otherwise. Rita was beautiful, and I could not figure out why she was still single. What must she be thinking about me? I gave my performance a six out of ten, but I did stick the landing after some detours. Rita seemed content. More dates followed, and we took up our new rhythm and routines.

Still no word from Ava.

Simon and I met for our usual lunch of fish and chips on Regency Street some weeks after I started dating Rita.

"You seem better," commented Simon, as we sat down in our usual booth.

"I guess so," I responded, but not really sure what that meant. "I think a better word is different…"

"Okay, 'different'…let's go from there…"

"Rita is really a very nice woman."

"Oh, wait, wait… "a nice woman"? Don't even tell me more, mate," Simon was shaking his head disapprovingly as he dove into his cod.

"What I mean is that I am just not sure. I don't want to hurt her. Some days it's like Ava is completely out of sight, out of mind. And just when I feel free, something reminds me of her. Or I miss something about her that I just can't seem to capture with Rita. There's been too much water under the bridge for me to move on just yet."

"You're the only one who knows what or who is best for you. All I know is that life is too short to be without someone

Finding Victoria

who loves you and makes you happy. No matter what it takes. Trust me, I know," said Simon, who was dousing his chips in ketchup.

He continued. "When I met Bernie, I told her something… The woman you truly love will be like that comfortable jersey one cannot part with. It's all new in your twenties, and you enjoy it. By your thirties, it's showing some wear, but still a mainstay item in your wardrobe and vibrant. By your forties, it becomes second nature to grab it from your wardrobe; it's reliable. In your fifties, people expect to see you wearing it; it is part of your identity. In your sixties and seventies? The idea of being without it is heartbreaking. If that makes sense to you, it might help you move forward."

All I was certain of was that my heart was still shattered and no temporary glue was going to hold it together, not yet. But there had been progress I could not ignore. I was new and improved.

Simon carried on with the usual conversation of politics, football, and grousing about the state of the world. No further discussion of women, no need. My therapy session was free and over.

And then the unthinkable happened. When I arrived home, Ava was sitting in the kitchen with a cup of coffee and a suitcase beside her. She had been crying. My heart was in my throat.

She asked, "Can we talk now?"

Finding Victoria

EPILOGUE

In writing this book, I had many moments of rediscovery …Victoria moments, in a way. One afternoon, I blew the dust off a leather satchel filled with writings I had saved since college. Some pieces were incomplete, just thoughtful phrases, quotes, or vivid descriptions scrawled on faded restaurant placemats, scraps of hotel stationery, or old mail envelopes. This is not too unusual among writers, I suppose. When you get a good idea, it needs to be written down immediately. And it's not unheard of to keep a pad of paper and pen next to your bed in case that vivid dream or eureka moment hits.

American writer F. Scott Fitzgerald's truncated musings and random observations were even gathered in a publication by editor Matthew Bruccoli in *The Notebooks of F. Scott Fitzgerald*. That's all the book was…no stories, no novel…just his fragmented notes. They were even categorized using over twenty topics. Sadly, I am not that organized.

As I sifted through my own scraps, many insights suspended me in a state of sincere disbelief that I had even written them, not so much because they were profound, but just that they were coming from a creative and spiritual place in me that I had ignored for so long and did not recognize. The many years that

Finding Victoria

had passed rendered the writings unfamiliar to me, but, surprisingly, here I was returning to them, and I eagerly found they only whetted my appetite for more. I was inspired again.

So, you and I are back to where we started…moments…emotions…ones that inspire, that spark, that reignite. And I plan to continue my visits to London (and elsewhere) to find *Victoria* again and again, as I hope you will find your Victoria. Perhaps one day our paths will cross?

ABOUT THE AUTHOR

Adelaide Rix is an American writer with an affinity for anything British and who enjoys many favorite London haunts. *Finding Victoria* has been a concept written in her head for several decades. She thanks her parents for their lifetime support and encouragement to pursue creative projects.

Rix continues to find her Victoria through her travels and daily experiences, always interested in the life stories of others, too. The love of her two grown children fuels her to live life to the fullest and to show gratitude every day.

Follow Adelaide Rix on Youtube, X, and adelaiderix.com. Watch for upcoming books! More to come…

Finding Victoria

All proceeds from this book will be donated to
Parkinson's UK
https://www.parkinsons.org.uk/

In aid of
Parkinson's UK

We don't wait for change, we make it happen. We believe that together we'll find a cure. But that's not all we're working for. We campaign for better health and care, fund research into groundbreaking new treatments, and run life-changing support services.

Families, volunteers, campaigners, fundraisers, scientists, health and care workers. We're a powerful community united by one mission: improving life with Parkinson's.

People's Trust for Endangered Species
https://ptes.org/

people's trust for endangered species

Our wildlife is disappearing. We are in danger of losing animals like red squirrels, dormice, and hedgehogs from Britain forever. There is nothing natural or inevitable about the alarming rate at which we are losing animals and their living landscapes. It can be stopped. That is why People's Trust for Endangered Species exists. For nearly 50 years, our ground-breaking research has resulted in practical conservation action across the world, targeted where it is most needed and where it will have maximum impact. Everyone can play a part, and together we can bring the wild back to life.

Finding Victoria

Finding Victoria

Finding Victoria

Printed in Dunstable, United Kingdom